Three of Hearts

KATHLEEN DUEY lives in California with the man she loves. Now that her sons are taller than she is, she spends most of her time researching and writing her two historical series, AMERICAN DIARIES and SURVIVAL! Her love of history and her appreciation for the courage of the people who settled and shaped America continue to grow.

KAREN A. BALE lives in California with her husband. She has nineteen-year-old twins who are beginning to make their way in the world. She has researched and written historical novels for twenty years. She enjoys the process of finding out why the past is so important to the present.

Three of Hearts

Kathleen Duey and Karen A. Bale

AN AVON CAMELOT BOOK

AVON BOOKS, INC.
1350 Avenue of the Americas
New York, New York 10019

Copyright © 1998 by Kathleen Duey and Karen A. Bale
Published by arrangement with the authors
Visit our website at **http://www.AvonBooks.com**
Library of Congress Catalog Card Number: 98-92781
ISBN: 0-380-78720-2

First Avon Camelot Printing: August 1998

CAMELOT TRADEMARK REG. U.S. PAT. OFF. AND IN OTHER COUNTRIES, MARCA REGISTRADA, HECHO EN U.S.A.

Printed in the U.S.A.

OPM   10   9   8   7   6   5   4   3   2   1

To the magic of friendship.

Three of Hearts

Chapter 1

Elsa Linstrom sat up in bed and stretched, yawning. Her back ached and the skin across her knuckles was cracked open. She knew her mother was exhausted, too, so it would do no good to complain. They had spent the last week rubbing beeswax into wood floors, scouring chamber pots, washing bed linens, and beating dust from the carpets at Miss Heatherton's Academy for Young Ladies. Today would be different but no easier. This was the first day of school.

Elsa dressed quickly, smoothing the skirt of her worn, yellow plaid dress. She jerked her hairbrush through her hair, impatient with the tangles. Her mother gently took the brush from her.

"Your hair is beautiful, Elsa. The color of honey. You should take care of it."

Elsa scuffed one foot and then the other on the planked floor as her mother braided her hair, trying to position the wads of paper in the toes of her shoes.

1

She'd only had them a month. They were her tenth birthday gift from her mother. They weren't as loose for her now as they had been the day her mother had given them to her. Her feet must be growing.

Elsa clenched her fists and winced from the pain of her lye-burned skin. Her mother's hands were always raw, a permanent, angry red from the lye soap they used for daily cleaning at the school. Elsa knew her own hands would be the same way.

She took a deep breath. This was her third year working with her mother at Miss Heatherton's Academy for Young Ladies. The first day of school was always the hardest for her. This year's girls would arrive in fine carriages, their soft leather shoes peeking from beneath their hooped skirts. They would have full, lace-trimmed sleeves, every one of them looking like an illustration in Godey's Lady's Book. Elsa stomped her foot. The wad of paper had shifted and she tried to work it back into place with her toes.

"Hush, don't wake your brother," Elsa's mother whispered. "He came in late last night."

Elsa looked aside. Did her mother think she couldn't hear Karl when he stumbled in, smelling like Mississippi River mud and singing tavern songs? Karl was twenty now. He should have been helping support them since Father had died, but he was too lazy to hold onto a job. All he ever wanted to do was argue with his friends about whether President Buchanan would be reelected or not—or whether there was going to be a war.

Elsa's mother reached out and touched her cheek. "Dress warm. It's a chilly morning."

Obediently Elsa lifted her brown wool shawl from its peg on the wall and wrapped it around her shoulders.

She opened the door and led the way out. She could hear the voices of the dock workers as they made their way down to the levee. There would already be steamboats tied up at the wharves, stacked with cargo. The stewards would be pacing, impatient, shouting at the stevedores to unload quickly. They wanted to refill their cargo decks and be on their way back downriver before noon.

As Elsa waited for her mother, she shrugged her shawl higher on her shoulders. It was still dark. Her mother shut the door quietly and came down the steps. As they started walking briskly along Sixth Street, Elsa could hear the familiar early morning sounds. There was the heavy clanging as the men at the Excelsior Stove Works down on Main Street stacked great sheets of iron. A distant steamboat whistle somewhere upriver set off Mrs. O'Cleary's roosters. A milk cow bawled. Elsa and her mother picked their way across the muddy street. The city of St. Louis was beginning to wake up.

Elsa's mother had always insisted on leaving early. She would never use the new Missouri Railway streetcars, Elsa was sure. They had never even gotten onto the horse drawn cars that clopped up and down nearly every downtown street. Elsa's mother didn't trust them to keep on schedule—nor would she waste money when they could rise early and walk.

Elsa didn't mind. This was the best part of her day. The city was still quiet, the silent brick buildings standing shoulder to shoulder. There were a few other people walking down Sixth, but not many. None of the businesses were open yet—a blacksmith was just now building his forge fire.

Elsa loved the way St. Louis rose above the river.

She loved looking back at the wide, brown Mississippi. There were two steamboats coming in this morning, their paddle wheels churning at the water. Their lacy upper decks and smokestacks reminded her of the fancy cakes her mother baked for the girls at the academy.

They walked fast. Elsa could hear the earliest songbird beginning to sing as she and her mother turned up Biddle Street, leaving most of the factories behind. This morning as they climbed the Biddle Street hill toward Eighth, Elsa loosened the shawl around her shoulders. It was only the end of August and the damp chill was delicious. By midday the weather would be muggy. In the kitchen at Miss Heatherton's it'd be almost unbearably hot and steamy.

Elsa had to hurry to keep up with her mother. As they passed St. Joseph's German Male School on the corner of Eleventh and Biddle, Elsa noticed that the kitchen lights were on. Her mother knew Mrs. Conger, the brusque, ill-tempered cook at St. Joseph's. She lived a little bit east of them, toward the river. Sometimes Mrs. Conger joined them along the way. She talked constantly, and Elsa always resented the intrusion of her sharp German accent into the cool and quiet of their morning walk.

Elsa was breathing hard when they reached the top of the hill near Sixteenth. From there the street leveled out, so her mother walked even faster. By the time they entered the gates of Miss Heatherton's Academy for Young Ladies Elsa's cheeks were warm and flushed.

Sparrows jabbered high in the oak trees that shaded the east side of the old mansion. Elsa followed her mother up the stone steps of the side porch that Miss Heatherton used as a servants' entrance.

Elsa hung her shawl on the brass hooks just inside the back door. Without being told she went outside to the chopping block and began to split the day's kindling. She carried in an armload and started the fires in both stoves. She dumped the water from the pan beneath the icebox and checked to see how much of the ice block had melted. This was the second day. It was more than half gone. Elsa set about filling the milk pitchers and cutting the slabs of butter. The syrup pitchers were sticky, so she wiped them off using the soapy water her mother had left in the washbasin the night before.

"I hear the bell," Elsa's mother said suddenly. "Do we need ice?"

Elsa nodded and ran out the door, turning toward the back entrance and the rutted drive that ran past the stables. The ice wagon driver saw her waving her apron and guided his slow-footed mare onto the drive. The silver bell wired to the driver's bench jangled madly as the wagon bounced. Elsa walked beside the wagon, enjoying the excuse to be outdoors.

The iceman used big steel tongs to lift the block of ice from the sawdust. With quick, practiced movements, he scraped it clean, then carried it into the kitchen as Elsa held the door open. He slid the heavy, frozen block into the ridged ice bin, then closed the icebox doors. Elsa watched him leave, leaning out the door.

"Elsa?"

"Yes, Mama." She went back to work.

By six-thirty it was stifling hot in the kitchen and they had propped open the back door. Elsa lifted her apron to her face, wiping the beads of sweat away. For a second she looked out at the early sunlight falling across the soft, green lawn.

5

"Elsa, don't stop. It'll scorch."

Without answering, Elsa gripped the handle of the large wooden spoon again. Her arms ached from stirring the heavy porridge.

"Is the dining hall ready?"

Elsa nodded. "I did that last night. You checked it."

Elsa's mother nervously tucked her blond hair back beneath her lace cap. "There are a hundred women who would like to have this position. There are so many out of work now, so many factories have closed down."

"Miss Heatherton likes you, Mama." Elsa glanced back out the door. Across the lawn she could see the high stone wall that blocked the view of Twenty-sixth Street. The grass looked impossibly green and inviting, like the grounds of a fairy-tale castle. She wondered what it would be like to run across it barefoot, a white, lacy gown billowing behind her.

"How is everything going in here?"

Elsa jerked her head back at the sound of Miss Heatherton's voice. She was a tall, elegant-looking woman who always wore dark dresses and pinned her auburn hair back tightly. Elsa felt herself straighten instinctively as Miss Heatherton came closer.

"Everything is fine, Miss Heatherton," Elsa's mother replied, her voice soft. "The muffins are in the oven, and I have batter for hotcakes. Elsa is stirring the porridge."

"Very good," Miss Heatherton said as she looked into the large pot. Then she straightened. "Remember, the girls will be arriving at seven, Lilia. Breakfast should be on the table promptly at seven-thirty."

"Yes, ma'am," Elsa's mother replied as Miss Heatherton disappeared through the swinging door that led to the dining hall.

Once she was gone, Elsa's mother turned. "That's enough stirring." She slid the porridge pot away from the firebox to the coolest part of the iron stove top. "Are you sure the napkins are all folded properly?"

"I'll check again if you want me to."

"No, that's all right. It's best if you start peeling potatoes for the noontime stew."

Frowning, Elsa went out the back door and down the steps. She hesitated by the root cellar doors, looking toward the Biddle Street gates. It wouldn't be long before the carriages began arriving, carrying girls dressed like princesses in books. Some would be shy and some would be giggling. None of them would ever have peeled potatoes in her life.

"It's not fair!" Matty Green stomped her shiny new shoes on the floorboards of the borrowed carriage. She flicked her ginger-colored braid back over her shoulder. "Why do I have to go? Why can't I just stay with you, Pa?"

"We've been over this a dozen times, Matty," Ben Green said to his daughter. "I'm on the river too much. You can't get proper schooling on a riverboat."

Matty fought with her stiff, starched petticoats, turning toward her father. "Lafayette teaches me. I've learned lots of things from him."

Matty's father shook his head. "Lafayette is a card dealer, Matty, a gambler."

"But I like him."

"I'm not arguing that, I'm just saying he's not a proper teacher."

7

"Then you could do it."

"I'd like you to get a better education than I can give you. Besides, you need to be around other girls," her father said, snapping the reins against the horse's back. He pointed. "Look there, Matty. I'm not a religious man, but it seems to me if God had a house that's what it would be like."

Matty studied the polished columns of the cathedral. She thought it was the most beautiful building in St. Louis. She let her eyes drift upward, tracing the shape of the spire. The early sun lit the gilt ball and cross that sat atop it. As Matty stared, spellbound, the cathedral's bells began to chime. She was used to hearing them from the hurricane deck of her father's steamboat when they were docked down on Front Street. But being this close, the metallic ring was almost deafening.

As the horse pulled them past the cathedral, Matty looked back. From here, she could see the face of the clock set into the tower. It was six-forty-five. In fifteen minutes, they would arrive at Miss Heatherton's Academy for Young Ladies.

"I'm going to hate it." Matty glanced up at her father. If he had heard her, he was ignoring her. Matty squirmed on the driver's bench. "I really don't want to go, Pa."

"I just want you to be able to make your own way in the world. Your mother, God bless her, was a good woman. If she hadn't died when you were born, I'm sure we would have had a good life together. But if I had died instead of her, I'm not sure what she would have done. You remember the Panic last year? Some men lost everything. That could happen to me." Ben Green shook his head. "Then there's all this talk about

8

secession. There's going to be a war, Matty. And when it comes, I don't want you on the river with me.''

Matty looked up at her father. He was always saying that war was about to come—but it never did. ''I won't know how to act around those girls, Pa.''

He smiled. ''Maybe not at first, but you'll learn.''

''I've seem them with their hoop skirts so wide they knock over furniture. And their stupid little parasols—''

Matty's father tugged gently at her braid. ''Try to remember not to swear like a dockhand every time you stub your toe and things will probably be easier for you.''

Matty didn't answer. She pulled at the fingers of the white gloves her father had made her wear.

''Here we are.''

Matty looked up and saw a high stone wall. The spiked iron gates had been pulled open, and as the carriage turned up the tree-lined drive, Matty stared at the imposing brick facade. She was going to be miserable here. She knew it.

Francesca de Larmo sat on the smooth leather carriage seat, her head high, her gloved hands folded on the lap of her blue silk dress. Her mother was telling her yet again how wonderful Miss Heatherton's Academy for Young Ladies was and how many of the city's best families were sending their daughters there. ''Juliana Sabin, two of the Smith girls, and . . .'' Francesca's mother paused until Francesca looked up. ''Clarice Laraby!''

Francesca smiled to please her mother but she was only half listening. She *was* excited about going to school. She loved it when her brother's tutor let her listen in. Reading her father's history books was like escaping into another life where things were important and people had real adventures. Sometimes she even wrote stories about ancient Greece in her diary.

As the driver pulled the team of matched black geldings into an abrupt right turn onto Biddle Street the carriage swayed, and Francesca heard her mother take in a startled little breath. "Oh, I do wish Henry would be more careful. I have half a mind to speak to your father about him. Perhaps he belongs back at field work after all."

"Henry is nice, Mother."

Francesca looked out her window as her mother adjusted her skirt hoops, scooting forward on the seat. "There it is!" Her mother giggled like a girl.

Francesca watched as the stone wall slid past. The carriage swayed again as Henry guided the team through the gates. A moment later, the carriage stopped. The geldings tossed their heads, making the brass harness buckles jingle.

Francesca's mother leaned close. "Mary Burton Harrison told me that Miss Heatherton is somehow connected to the New York Cavendishes—a second cousin or some such thing. She inherited this place. Can you imagine?"

Francesca nodded. She had heard the story several times. Miss Heatherton had converted the old mansion into a boarding school four years before. She had almost lost it when her bank failed, but old family friends had extended her credit.

Just then, Henry opened the carriage door and offered Francesca his arm. She thanked him when he helped her down, and she waited for her mother. "The second carriage with the young mistress' trunks will arrive momentarily, madam," Henry said in his soft deep voice.

Francesca's mother was beaming at her. "Are you ready?"

Francesca stared at the handsome brick building, its wide pillared porch laced with honeysuckle growing up white latticework trellises. She took a deep breath and nodded. Her mother swept her forward, her silk gown rustling.

Elsa peeked through the white swinging door into the dining hall. Miss Heatherton had all of the girls assembled in a straight line. The room was spotlessly clean. The tall green-glass vase at the foot of the ornate staircase shone like water in the sun. The parents had finally left. Now Miss Heatherton would give her Welcome Day speech. She was very stern. She always told the girls what she expected from them, and even the snootiest of them paid attention.

"Is she done speaking?" Elsa's mother asked from behind her.

"No, she hasn't even begun," Elsa whispered. "She's just standing there with her arms crossed, staring at all of them."

"I don't understand why this interests you so much. You hear this every year."

Elsa didn't try to explain. How often did she get to see rich, spoiled girls looking nervous? Elsa's eyes skipped from one girl to the next. She recognized Clarice Laraby's pale, freckled face and sighed. Clarice was a troublemaker. Elsa looked down the line again. There were only five or six new ones this year. Near the window that looked out onto the front porch there was a pretty girl with thick, black hair wearing a beautiful blue dress. She stood perfectly straight and her dark eyes were focused intently on Miss Heatherton as she spoke.

"Excuse me, miss," Miss Heatherton said suddenly. Elsa watched her walk toward a girl with a ginger-colored braid. She was standing with one foot atop the other, her hands locked behind her back. She was staring at the painting on the wall above the sideboard. It was obvious she wasn't listening to Miss Heatherton.

"Excuse me . . . ?" Miss Heatherton raised her voice and the girl looked at her.

"Yes?"

Elsa took a quick little breath. Even she knew it was proper etiquette to call Miss Heatherton by her name or by "ma'am."

Miss Heatherton seemed to tower over the girl. "What's your name, young lady?"

"Matty Green."

"Do you know where you are, Miss Green?"

"Yes."

"Would you mind telling all of us?"

Elsa watched as Matty Green shrugged her shoulders indifferently. "Miss Heatherton's Academy for Young Ladies."

"And do you know what we do here at the academy?"

"Not really. My father made me come."

Elsa had never heard anyone speak like this to Miss Heatherton. She held her breath.

"Would I be correct in assuming, Miss Green, that your father loves you?"

"Yes."

Elsa noticed that for the first time Matty Green didn't meet Miss Heatherton's eyes.

"Do you think your father sent you here to punish you, Miss Green?"

"No, I don't think so."

"Why do you think he sent you here?"

Matty Green shrugged. "He wants me to get an education."

"Don't you want an education, Miss Green? Wouldn't you like to put that sharp tongue and quick mind of yours to good use?"

Elsa watched as Matty Green looked up at Miss Heatherton. "Yes." She swallowed. "Ma'am."

Nodding to acknowledge Matty's answer, Miss Heatherton began her regular Welcome Day speech. At the end of it she gestured toward the tables. "You may all sit down. Breakfast will be served now."

Elsa eased the door closed. "They're sitting down, Mama."

"Here," Elsa's mother said, pulling a platter of steaming hotcakes from the oven. "Take these in and remember to answer politely if any of the girls speak to you."

Elsa took a deep breath. This was the part she hated the most. On the first day it seemed as though all the girls had to stare at her, noticing her worn dress, her scuffed shoes.

"Elsa? Do as you're told."

"Yes, Mama," Elsa said dutifully, backing through the swinging door into the dining hall. There were two long tables placed in the center of the room across from the big windows that faced east. Miss Heatherton sat at the table closest to the wide, curving stairway that led to the girls' rooms on the second floor. Elsa set the platter in front of Miss Heatherton. Then she went to the polished oak sideboard to fetch the maple syrup and the butter dishes.

"Thank you, Elsa."

"You're welcome, ma'am."

Miss Heatherton took Elsa's wrist and gently turned her around. "Girls, this is Elsa. She helps her mother, Mrs. Linstrom, with the cooking. They will be preparing wonderful meals for all of us."

Elsa saw Matty Green smiling at her from the other end of the table and quickly looked away. "May I go, ma'am?"

"Yes, of course."

Elsa's mother was carrying in the second platter of hotcakes as Elsa went back into the kitchen. For a few minutes they bustled back and forth bringing the white porcelain milk pitchers and the bowls of hot porridge. Elsa set the sugar bowl down directly in front of Matty.

"Thank you, Elsa."

"You're welcome," Elsa said shyly. She looked up to see Clarice Laraby glaring at her. Matty was still smiling, but Elsa turned abruptly and went back into the kitchen. Clarice's rudeness had always made her angry—but what could she do about it?

The long first day passed slowly. After supper Elsa lit the gas lamps. She polished the table until it shone, then replaced the delicate lace runner and the Waterford crystal fruit bowl that Miss Heatherton had inherited from her aunt. The center of the other table was reserved for a silver candle tree.

Elsa stood back, admiring her work. The dining hall

was immaculate. Even the sideboard, which would be covered with serving dishes again in the morning, looked neat and polished with its crystal decanter and silver tea service. The flickering gas lamp made the flowered wallpaper shimmer.

Elsa imagined herself having meals with the other girls, giggling and sharing secrets with friends. She would wear a green dimity dress with a full skirt, and she would carefully lift her hoops so that she could sit more gracefully. Miss Heatherton would make a fuss over how well she had read aloud in class that day, and all the other girls would look at her with envy.

"Are you finished, Elsa?"

Elsa's daydream evaporated at the sound of her mother's tired voice. "Yes, Mama."

"It's time to go, then. We still have our own supper to cook."

Elsa retreated into the kitchen and took her shawl from the wall peg, wrapping it around her shoulders. She waited outside the back door as her mother blew out the lamps and closed the door. Then they started home. As they walked down the drive, Elsa looked back. In one of the upstairs windows she could see Matty Green sitting on the window seat. Matty looked warm and happy. Elsa shivered in the chilly evening air.

"Come along, Elsa. Don't dawdle. It's a long walk home."

15

Chapter 2

$\mathcal{L}$ike she had every night since she had arrived at Miss Heatherton's Academy for Young Ladies, Matty sat on the window seat, pulling her long cotton nightgown over her knees. It was foggy again tonight, and she couldn't see the Mississippi River, couldn't see the lights of the paddle wheelers as they made their way upriver. She hummed a tune that her father had taught her. It was a song her friend Lafayette sang all the time.

"Must you sit there every night and do that? It's a silly song, anyway."

Matty turned to look at her roommate, Francesca de Larmo. This was the largest room at Miss Heatherton's, and it still wasn't nearly large enough for Francesca. Her side of the room was lined with trunks, and her dresses almost filled their wardrobe. The day before, two servants had come to bring Francesca her own little writing desk from her room at home. That's where she was sitting now, her leather-bound journal open before

16

her, their Astral lamp turned up high enough so that Matty could smell the fishy odor of the burning whale oil.

Matty sighed. All Francesca ever did was write in her stupid journal and order people around. Matty propped her chin on her knees and hummed louder.

Francesca shook her head. "Of all the girls in this academy, why did Miss Heatherton put me with you?"

"Maybe she thought it would be good for you."

"I'm going to request that she move you to another room."

"Move yourself," Matty said stubbornly. "I like this room." The only good thing about this school was the east-facing window that allowed Matty to see the river sometimes. She started her song over.

"I hate that tune."

"I don't care," Matty replied, looking back out the window. She heard Francesca scrape her chair back. A moment later Francesca blew out the lamp.

Matty sat in the darkness, feeling the cool air on her cheeks. She knew it wouldn't be long before Francesca began crying. She cried every night. Matty wrapped her arms around her knees, resting her chin on top. Francesca's crying made her feel even more sad. Matty wanted nothing more than to go home—to be on the river with her father. She hated it here at Miss Heatherton's and she knew it wouldn't get any better. She stared out into the night for a moment longer, then went to bed.

Elsa sighed. It was almost time for the ten o'clock break. The girls would be finishing up their history lesson. When she could, Elsa liked to overhear Miss Heatherton's lectures, but this morning it was impossible. She had to polish the dark walnut bannister. When she heard the girls come out of the classrooms she knelt, facing away from them, cleaning the base of the ornate balustrade. She didn't look up as the girls began to file into the dining hall below.

"There's Elsa."

Elsa recognized Clarice's voice. Without raising her eyes she knew Annabelle Gregor and Caroline Farley would be with her. They always were.

"Why don't you answer me, Elsa?"

Elsa murmured politely, and moved up another few steps, rubbing the carved balustrade with her polishing rag.

"I think she's being rude."

Elsa stood abruptly and went to the top of the stairs, intending to work her way back down. She knelt and started polishing again, hoping Clarice would lose interest. Sometimes she did.

"Could you help me with something, Elsa?"

Startled, Elsa rocked back on her heels. Clarice was standing on the step below her. Her shoes had been nearly silent on the thick carpet.

"Help you with what?"

"I want to show you something in my room. You didn't clean it well enough last time."

Resigned, Elsa stood up and followed Clarice and her friends. At the top of the stairway they rounded the corner and passed Miss Heatherton's living quarters. Then they turned down the main hall; there were rooms on both sides. Clarice opened the first door on the right.

18

"Come inside," Clarice said, leading the way. Annabelle and Caroline flounced past. Elsa looked down the hall, hesitating. Miss Heatherton and her mother were downstairs. "What do you want to show me?"

"Come over here," Clarice said.

Elsa took a few tentative steps into the room. "I have work to do, miss." She glanced back toward the door.

"Look at me when I'm speaking to you. Don't be so rude, or I'll have to tell Miss Heatherton. We just wanted to ask you something." Clarice smiled at her friends and then back at Elsa. "How old is that dress? And where did you get those shoes? They couldn't possibly be yours. I mean, they look three sizes too big."

Elsa felt her cheeks burn as the girls dissolved into laughter. For a moment she couldn't move. Then she whirled and ran from the room. She hurried down the stairs and across the dining hall, refusing to look down at her shoes.

Matty chewed on the end of her pencil. Miss Heatherton was lecturing on Greek myths, but Matty wasn't listening. She stared at Francesca instead. Her roommate was dressed in soft green silk, full petticoats peeking from beneath the hem. Her dark hair was braided on both sides and pulled back in an ornate comb. Matty had to admit that Francesca was pretty. She had perfect posture and she seemed to be an excellent student. She never stopped taking notes.

"Miss Green? Do you know the answer?"

Matty looked toward Miss Heatherton. "I'm sorry, I didn't hear the question."

"That's what I thought," Miss Heatherton said sharply. "Miss de Larmo, can you tell us?"

Francesca didn't hesitate. "The Greek goddess of war is Athena. She is also the goddess of wisdom."

"Can you tell us anything else about her?"

Matty watched as Francesca nodded and smiled slightly, obviously delighted to be able to show off.

"Athena sprang fully grown from Zeus's head." Francesca looked around at the other girls. "Zeus was her father."

Miss Heatherton gave her an approving nod. "Thank you very much, Francesca. It's good to see a student who takes her studies seriously."

Matty rolled her eyes. One of these days she would have to let Francesca know that she wasn't the only one who had read a few Greek myths. Before Miss Heatherton could resume her lecture, there was a quiet knock on the door. She went to answer it.

Matty could see Elsa standing in the hallway, her arms full of small boxes. "My mother said to bring these. Where should I put them, ma'am?"

"On the front table, Elsa. Would you please open the box containing the steel pens and inkwells and set them out?" Miss Heatherton looked back at the class. "Starting today, you girls will do all your work in ink, in a clean, precise hand. If you smudge, spill or smear your ink, you will be asked to do it over again."

Matty barely heard Miss Heatherton. She was watching Elsa. The serving girl kept glancing at Miss Heatherton, looking at each box, running her fingers over the painted letters. When Elsa opened one of the boxes and quickly closed it, blushing, then opened another, Matty was puzzled. Then she realized why—Elsa couldn't read.

Matty wondered if anyone else had noticed, and hoped Elsa would find the pens and ink soon. When she opened the next box and pulled out the inkwells and a handful of steel pens, Matty breathed a sigh of relief. She watched Elsa turn and go out the door.

"Miss Green, are you daydreaming again?"

"No, I'm not," Matty replied, meeting Miss Heatherton's stern eyes.

"Then perhaps you'd like to tell me about Hercules."

Matty cleared her throat. "Hercules was the son of Zeus and a mortal woman. Zeus's wife, Hera, hated Hercules and wanted to destroy him, but Zeus loved his son and always made sure that he was safe." Matty cast a look toward Francesca. Her eyes were wide as Matty went on. "He performed twelve great labors for his cousin, the king of Argos."

"I don't suppose you could name a few of Hercules' labors?" Miss Heatherton asked.

Matty sat up straighter. "He killed the Nemean lion, the Hydra, he captured a stag and a wild boar in the Arcadian Mountains, he cleaned King Augeas's stables in one day—"

"Quite impressive, Matty. I see you have done your reading."

"Thank you, ma'am." Matty felt smug. Her father had been reading Greek myths instead of bedtime stories to her since she could remember, and Hercules had always been one of her favorites.

"All right, girls. It's almost noon. We'll have our dinner now. Be back promptly at twelve-thirty."

Matty gathered her things and glanced over at Francesca, but she was already talking to a girl named Sally who giggled all the time. Juliana Sabin joined them, then three or four more girls. They left the room together.

Matty frowned. Francesca already knew every girl in the class; everyone wanted to be her friend. Matty pretended to go through her notes, waiting until the classroom was empty. Then she walked out alone.

Matty was starting to dread the free hour between supper and bedtime. She never knew what to do. This evening she could hear the piano from the hallway as she wandered toward the music room.

Turning to go in the door, she could see Francesca. Her skirts were spread over the bench, her back ramrod straight as she played "The Yellow Rose of Texas," lifting her hands dramatically at the end of each phrase. As always, she was surrounded by smiling girls. Four or five were leaning on the piano. Clarice Laraby was among them.

Matty sat in one of the chairs by the windows and looked around the room as Francesca ended the song and swung right into "The Old Grey Mare." Francesca knew all the newest songs, Mattie thought, pretending not to be interested.

Some of the girls were laughing over a match of cross questions; some were playing checkers. Juliana and a few others were working on their embroidery samplers. But the biggest group of all was clustered around the piano.

When Francesca finished, she stood up and walked dreamily toward the center of the room, the blue petticoats underneath her gray satin dress swaying gracefully as Annabelle began to play a simple waltz. Giggling, she began to waltz in the middle of the room and Matty watched as she glided around the polished floor, arms lifted to embrace an imaginary partner.

"You're such a graceful dancer, Francesca. Why don't you teach us all?" Theresa Bolton suggested.

Francesca smiled shyly as the girls gathered around her in a circle. Matty glanced toward the door, but it was too late.

"Will you join us, Matty?" Francesca asked.

She was smiling, but Matty was afraid Francesca would make fun of her. "No, thank you."

Clarice was frowning. "Oh, come on."

Matty stood up. "I said no, thank you."

Clarice shook her head. "Fine. But you ought to learn. It's obvious your mother never taught you anything about being ladylike."

Matty wasn't about to explain to Clarice that she'd never known her mother. Her father had said not to swear, but he hadn't said she had to let someone insult her.

"I wouldn't talk if I were you, Clarice," Matty said evenly. "With a face like yours, you're lucky Miss Heatherton didn't assign you a roommate out in the stable." There was astonished silence, then a scattering of giggles as what Matty had said was repeated around the room.

"You're a hateful person, Matty Green," Francesca said, taking Clarice's arm and leading her away.

Matty ignored the astonished stares of the other girls as she turned to leave. She went up the stairs as fast as her petticoats would allow. Closing the door of her room behind her she leaned on it for a moment, trying to calm down. Impatient to be free of her stays and petticoats, Matty changed into her nightclothes. Raising the window as high as it would go she sat on the window seat, looking out. A riverboat whistled in the distance, and her heart ached. All she wanted was to be back with her father and Lafayette.

Matty was startled out of her lonely thoughts by voices and muted laughter in the hall outside. Then the door opened and she could understand what the girls were saying.

"Good night, Francesca. Maybe we can dance again tomorrow evening."

"Good night."

Matty stared pointedly out the open window, ignoring the chill of the night air as Francesca shut the door and began her nightly ritual. The last thing Matty wanted to do was watch Francesca get ready for bed. She never did anything differently. Matty heard the wardrobe open and close as Francesca changed into her nightdress. Matty knew exactly what she would do next: wash her face, brush her hair one hundred times, then get into bed, propping herself up with her feather pillows. When Matty heard the scraping of a pen on paper she knew that Francesca was writing in her journal, as she did every night.

"Would you please close that window?" Francesca asked. "The cold air is bad for me."

Matty tapped one finger against the windowsill, trying to control her temper. "It's fresh air, and it's good for you."

"Please, Matty, shut the window!"

"No." Matty turned so that she was facing Francesca. "I'm not your servant. If you want it closed, you do it."

"Clarice is right about you."

Matty shrugged. "I don't care about her."

"All the girls think you're odd, Matty, and so do I."

Matty crossed the room and stood in front of Francesca. "How would you know? You never even talk to me. You'd rather write in that stupid journal. You're the most boring roommate anyone ever had."

"All you ever do is stare out the window and hum that awful song. You're the one who's boring."

"I can change that." Matty grabbed the journal from Francesca's hands and ran to the window; she dangled it outside.

"Don't you dare drop that, Matty Green."

"Give me one good reason."

"Because I told you not to."

Matty stared. Did Francesca think she was just going to obey her, like one of her housemaids? Raising the leather-bound book so that Francesca could see it clearly, Matty opened her hand and let it go.

Francesca brushed past her, leaning out the window. "Oh, Matty. How could you? I've had that journal since I was eight years old. It has all my secrets in it."

When Francesca turned around, Matty could see tears in her eyes. "I didn't know it meant that much to you."

"You don't care anything about anyone. You're selfish and mean."

"What about you? Your not happy unless everybody's admiring you. You're even friends with Clarice."

Francesca shook her head. "We just talk, that's all."

"About me."

"About everything. You'd know that if you'd ever join the rest of us, Matty."

"I don't even like these girls."

Francesca glanced out the window. "And you hate me."

"No, I don't. I just got angry, that's all. I have a bad temper." She gestured out the window. "It isn't ruined—it's just down there."

"But what if Miss Heatherton finds it and reads it? I've said some things about her."

Matty turned. "You have? What?"

Francesca nodded. "I said I thought her face looked like an old prune."

Matty laughed. "Well, I guess we can't let her find it, then." She sat on the windowsill, looking at Francesca. Then she turned, ducking her head beneath the raised sash and lifting her legs over the wooden casing. The brick wall felt cold and rough on the backs of her thighs and the honeysuckle vine tickled her bare feet.

"What are you doing?"

"I'm going to get your journal."

"Matty, don't—you can't do that."

Matty almost laughed. "It's a lot easier than climbing the fretwork between the boiler deck and the hurricane deck on my pa's boat."

"Matty, you'll get hurt."

"No, I won't, Francesca. It's my fault, and I'll go get it." Matty turned, supporting her weight on her hands, so that her stomach was against the sill. She lowered herself a little, feeling for the top of the trellis with her feet. As soon as she found a foothold, she eased herself onto the trellis, letting go of the sill with one hand, then the other. As she moved downward into the darkness the honeysuckle vine caught at her night-gown. At the bottom the grass felt cool between her toes and she stood for a moment enjoying it.

"Matty, hurry." Francesca's frantic whisper came from above.

Matty searched for the journal. There was a half moon casting faint shadows on the lawn. She finally found Francesca's book a few feet farther away from the vine than she had thought it would be. Reluctant to go back inside, she slowly climbed the trellis and scrambled over the window sill.

"Here," she said, handing over the journal. She brushed the honeysuckle leaves from her nightgown.

"Thank you."

"You're welcome."

"You have grass on your feet."

Matty swiped a hand over the bottom of each foot.

"I've never seen a girl do anything like that," Francesca said, sitting on Matty's bed.

Matty sat next to her. "It's not that high, Francesca. Don't you have trees where you live?"

"Of course."

"Haven't you ever climbed one of them?"

"No, my mother would never permit that."

Matty shook her head, tucking her feet beneath her. "How could you not try it at least once? It's fun."

"I'm not allowed, that's all." Francesca walked to her desk and put the journal inside. "We should probably blow out the lamp. Miss Heatherton will be checking pretty soon."

"I guess so." Matty got under her covers and slid down between the cool linen sheets as Francesca put out the lamp. She stared up at the dark ceiling. "I'm sorry I did that, Francesca."

"You went and got it. It's all right."

"Francesca?"

"Yes?"

"What would you do if you couldn't read or write?" There was a long silence. "I don't know."

"You know Elsa?"

"Who?"

"The cook's daughter."

"Oh, yes."

"I don't think she can read." Francesca didn't answer, so Matty went on. "Remember when she brought boxes into the lesson room and Miss Heatherton told her to get out the steel pens?"

"What about it?"

"I could tell she couldn't read the boxes. She had to look inside to see what was there."

"That's not uncommon with servants, Matty."

"I wonder why Miss Heatherton doesn't teach her."

"Because she's not here to learn how to read, Matty, she's here to help in the kitchen."

Matty propped herself up on one elbow. "We could teach her to read, Francesca."

"We can't, Matty. She's the cook's daughter."

"That doesn't matter."

Matty could hear the impatience in Francesca's voice. "Yes, it does. My father says that servants are harder to manage if they can read. Miss Heatherton wouldn't want us to."

"But it would be fun, Francesca."

Francesca made an impatient little sound. "You *are* odd, Matty, but I'm beginning to like you. Good night."

"Good night," Matty mumbled, still thinking about Elsa. After a long time Matty realized the room was silent. For the first night since they'd come to school, Francesca hadn't cried herself to sleep.

Chapter 3

After washing the morning dishes, Elsa took her bucket and mop to the upstairs hallway. Miss Heatherton liked the floors washed with a damp mop every other day and polished with beeswax and lemon oil once a month. Elsa worked quickly. She wanted to finish before the girls came out for their mid-morning break. She didn't want another encounter with Clarice.

Elsa made her way down the hallway, sliding the dampened mop along the wooden floor. She made sure it was properly wrung out so that no extra water remained. Miss Heatherton didn't want the oak planking warped or stained.

Elsa's arms ached, but she kept going, trying to ignore the smell of the heavy lye soap. She ran the mop around the base of the tall cabinet clock, then the brass plant stand that held Miss Heatherton's prized parlor palm tree. Once the hallway was finished, Elsa moved downstairs, the heavy bucket bumping against her leg.

She finished the entryway, the hall that ran past the lesson rooms, and finally the kitchen floor. She carried the dirty water outside and dumped it on the lawn.

As she came back in, her mother turned from the pot of soup she was stirring. "Have you dusted the music room?"

Elsa pushed her hair back from her forehead. "Not yet. I have to rinse the mop first."

"Leave it. I will do that. Miss Heatherton wanted the dusting done this morning."

Elsa stood the mop against the wall, then got the oily dust cloth from the pantry and went out the little side door that led directly into the ground-floor hallway. She could hear voices in the lesson room as she opened the music room door and slipped inside.

This was Elsa's favorite place in the school. It was a large room, almost as big as the dining hall. There was a drop-leaf table by the tall window where the girls normally sat and chatted. Elsa stood quietly, taking in the shiny mahogany piano, the lovely chairs with their fine needlework seats, and the glass-fronted cabinet containing Miss Heatherton's delicate figurines. She faced the tall bookcase filled with leather-bound volumes that Miss Heatherton allowed the girls to borrow. Elsa looked at them whenever she got the chance, even though she knew her mother would be angry if she found out. Some of them had beautiful pictures in them.

Elsa loved to dust this room. It seemed like the sun always shone brightly on the pretty rose wallpaper— like a garden. She started dusting the piano, running the cloth over the smooth dark wood. It always seemed like magic when someone sat at the bench and made beautiful music. As always, she wanted to press a key or two just to hear the sound, but didn't dare.

Elsa cleaned the drop-leaf table and the chairs, careful to get all the dust off the splats and rungs. She would have to come back to wipe the glass front of the cabinet that held Miss Heatherton's collection of figurines—the oil in the dust cloth would only streak it.

Elsa dusted the bookcase, careful not to get the oil on any of the leather bindings. Then she did the lowest shelves, where Miss Heatherton stored the checkerboards and domino sets the girls used in the evenings and on rainy days. She was moving the ornate chess set on the third shelf when she noticed a tiny corner of something showing from behind the bookcase.

Cautiously, Elsa wiped her oily hands on her apron, then reached back and touched the dark leather binding of a slim book. She carefully pulled it free and opened it. She flipped through the pages, recognizing a few of the letters of the alphabet. This was a primer. She had seen Miss Heatherton using it when her little nieces had visited. Elsa ran her fingers over the letters.

Elsa closed the book and held it tightly against her chest. With a book like this, she might be able to teach herself to read. She stood up. No one used this book now. No one had used it since last winter. She was almost certain that Miss Heatherton would not miss it if she borrowed it for a few days.

Trembling with nervousness, Elsa slipped the book underneath her apron, hugging it close. She picked up the dust cloth and stood by the door, listening to make sure the hall was empty before she went out. As she entered the kitchen, she heard water splashing and looked out the back door to see her mother at the pump, washing out the mop. Elsa looked around frantically, her eye coming to rest on the wood box. It was the perfect place. She was the only one who brought in the firewood. Elsa grabbed a clean towel from the drying rack and quickly wrapped the book, hiding it beneath the kindling in the box.

"I finished the music room, Mama," she said as her mother came in. Elsa tried to make her voice sound normal, but her heart was pounding. She had never lied to her mother before.

Her mother smiled. "Good, now you can take these soft ginger cakes in there. The girls are having a snack today. If they make a mess, we'll just have to clean it up again."

Elsa picked up the platter of sugar-speckled ginger cakes and carried them carefully into the music room. When she was just inside, she heard voices in the hall-way. She hesitated, then peeked back out the door. Girls were already coming down the hall. Some walked in pairs; others came more slowly, their heads close to-gether as they whispered to each other. Elsa hurried to set down the platter, but it was already too late to leave without being seen. The first few girls were coming into the music room.

Elsa stood to the side and they took no notice of her as they filed in. She watched as the pretty, dark-haired girl walked by, surrounded by friends. Clarice and her two friends walked in, stopping just inside the door. Matty Green came in alone. She smiled and Elsa smiled back. Elsa started to leave, nearly bumping into Clarice. Elsa froze for a second, then tried to go past them, but Clarice blocked her way.

"Where are you going?"

"I have to get back to the kitchen."

"But I want you to serve us first." Clarice looked at her friends. They smiled, and Elsa felt her cheeks flush.

"I'm not supposed to serve the cakes. Please let me pass."

Clarice wrinkled her brow then shook her head. "I think you should. The housemaids at home always serve dessert."

Elsa felt her embarrassment harden into anger, and it frightened her. She pressed her lips together to keep from saying something foolish.

"I'm going to tell Miss Heatherton about you." Clarice leaned close and Elsa fought an urge to push her away.

"Stop it, Clarice. It's not right to talk to her like that." It was Matty Green. Elsa watched, amazed, as Matty came to stand beside her.

Clarice bristled. "What would you know about servants, anyway?" She looked at her friends again. "Her father is a common riverboat captain, not a gentleman. Matty Green, the river rat."

Elsa touched Matty's shoulder. "It's all right."

Clarice leaned forward, taking Matty's hands. "Elsa and Matty. Best friends. Aren't they sweet?"

Without warning, Matty jerked her hands free, and Clarice stumbled backward, sitting down hard on her skirt hoops and starched petticoats. She began to cry.

Elsa looked at Matty. "You're going to get in trouble."

"I don't care."

"I'm sorry, miss," Elsa said to Clarice, "but Miss Heatherton says I am not supposed to wait on anyone except at mealtime."

Matty shot Elsa a glance and her face was tense, her mouth rigid, outlined in white. It took Elsa a moment

34

to realize that Matty wasn't upset—she was trying not to laugh.

Not daring to look at Clarice as she stepped around her, Elsa turned toward the kitchen. Clarice's wails rose behind her and Elsa knew Miss Heatherton would soon be in the music room.

"Is someone hurt?" her mother asked as she came in. Elsa shook her head and turned away, finally allowing herself to smile at the image of Clarice Laraby sitting on the floor, wailing like a baby.

Matty nervously scuffed her shoe along the wine-colored carpet. She'd been called into Miss Heatherton's office because of Clarice, she was sure. Miss Heatherton was writing something and had asked her to wait. Now there was nothing she could do but stand awkwardly, looking around the well-organized room.

The desk was long. Besides an Astral lamp, nothing cluttered the top. There were two wooden slat-back chairs, but Miss Heatherton had not invited Matty to sit down. As Matty watched, Miss Heatherton's pen scratched back and forth across the paper in an elegant, precise hand. She finally looked up. "Well? What do you have to say for yourself, Miss Green?"

Matty thought for a moment. She didn't want to blurt out something that would just make Miss Heatherton more angry. "Clarice was being mean to Elsa. Then she insulted me."

"So you thought it appropriate to push her down?"

"I didn't do that."

"That's not what some of the girls told me."

"She called me a name."

"I will not condone physical violence at this school."

35

Miss Heatherton held up a hand to stop Matty's response. "I don't want to hear about anything like this again."

"Yes, ma'am." Matty sighed.

Miss Heatherton folded her hands atop her desk. "However, I do think it quite commendable that you tried to protect Elsa. She is no one's servant; she works for this school. Be assured that I will have a talk with Clarice."

Matty met her eyes. "Thank you, ma'am."

"I've given some thought to your punishment. You will get up early tomorrow morning and help Elsa and Mrs. Linstrom prepare breakfast."

"Yes, ma'am."

"You will serve it as well."

Matty couldn't hide her shock. "Serve? In the dining room?"

"Yes. I'll make sure Clarice behaves."

"That's not fair, Miss Heatherton."

"On the contrary, I think it more than fair. I will not speak to your father this time. That will be all, Matty."

"But I don't know how to serve."

"Elsa's mother will show you. You'll need to be in the kitchen at six o'clock."

Matty started for the door but stopped when Miss Heatherton spoke again. "Matty."

"Yes, ma'am."

"As I said on the first day of school, you might think about putting that sharp tongue of yours to better use. Clarice is difficult, I admit. Obviously I do not permit name-calling, but I certainly don't mind a good battle of wits, Miss Green."

"Yes, ma'am." Matty closed the door behind herself and walked slowly down the hallway. Lost in thought, she turned toward her room, trying to figure out what Miss Heatherton meant. One thing was sure: Her father was going to be very upset with her if she got into more trouble.

Matty stopped in front of her own door. She could hear some of the other girls giggling, supposedly studying but really visiting and gossiping. It would be different in her room. Francesca would be doing her daily lessons or writing in her journal.

Matty opened the door. Francesca was at her writing desk, her left hand holding open a book, furiously copying something. She set down her pen.

"Did you get in trouble?"

Matty nodded, plopping onto her bed. "Miss Heatherton wasn't too happy with me."

"Is she going to send for your father?"

"No. But I have to help cook breakfast with Elsa and her mother tomorrow morning."

"Oh, my," Francesca muttered, a hand over her mouth.

"I have to serve it, too."

Francesca gasped. She got up from her desk and sat next to Matty on the bed. Matty squared her shoulders. "Elsa does it every day."

"But waiting on people . . . ?"

Matty shrugged. "I get my own dinner from the galley all the time. You're used to house servants. I'm not."

The tall clock began to strike eight. They jumped up and undressed, getting into their beds less than a minute before Miss Heatherton opened the door to check on them. Once she had gone, Matty lay awake, thinking. Clarice was mean and she got away with too much. The battle of wits was about to begin.

37

Elsa watched as Matty silently stirred the huge pot of oatmeal. It was very strange to have one of the girls in the kitchen. Matty had followed every order her mother had given her and not complained once, but Elsa could tell having Matty here made her mother uncomfortable.

Elsa's mother took the spoon from Matty's hands. "You're a good worker, Matty. I'll take over for now."

"No, ma'am. I can do it."

"I know you can. But we've finished everything early with your help. Elsa, pour some cold milk and each of you take one of those muffins outside. We'll start serving in a while."

"You're sure, Mama?"

"I'm sure."

Elsa followed Matty outside and they sat on the bottom step, eating in silence. Elsa knew she should say something to Matty but she didn't know what.

"It's nice out here," Matty said. "Quiet."

Elsa looked out at the gnarled limbs of the oak trees. The lawn was soft green in the early sunlight. "Sometimes I dream of running across the grass," she said softly.

"Why don't you?"

"I'm not allowed. If Miss Heatherton saw me, my mother might lose her job."

"Just for running on the grass?"

"I'm not a student." Elsa took a bite of the warm apple muffin then drank some milk. "I'm sorry you got into trouble."

"I'm not. It was worth seeing Clarice on the floor, wasn't it?" Matty leaned back, sticking her legs in the air and pulling the skirt of her dress up over her stockinged knees, thrashing her legs the way Clarice had.

38

Elsa giggled, her hand over her mouth. "You're funny, Matty."

"Miss Heatherton doesn't think so." Matty lifted her glass of milk.

Elsa hesitated, then spoke. "It's going to be hard for you today. You know Clarice will do something to make you angry."

Matty shrugged. "She can say whatever she wants. I'm not going to get in trouble again. If I do, Miss Heatherton will send for my father."

"Is your father strict?"

Elsa watched Matty laugh. "My father? Gosh, no. It's just that he wants me to do well here."

"It's time," Elsa's mother said from the doorway behind them.

"Yes, Mama," Elsa said, standing up.

Matty got to her feet and met Elsa's eyes. "Well, here we go, into the cave of the Gorgon."

Elsa wanted to ask Matty what she meant, but her mother was calling them from inside the kitchen. Matty grinned and Elsa smiled back at her.

Matty peeked into the dining room as Elsa's mother began ladling oatmeal into the deep blue bowls. Miss Heatherton sat at the head of the front table. Clarice sat at the other end.

"Ready now," Elsa's mother said.

They each took two bowls and went through the door into the dining hall.

"I'll do that one," Matty whispered, gesturing with her chin. "That way you don't have to worry about Clarice the witch this morning."

Elsa shook her head, but Matty didn't give her time

to protest. She veered toward the front table, walking carefully, her head held high. She refused to look at Clarice and concentrated on serving, surprised at how heavy the oatmeal bowls were.

Matty imitated Elsa, carrying the bowls two at a time, going back and forth to the kitchen. Clarice whispered a few things to her friends and threw Matty some nasty looks, but other than that, nothing much happened. Miss Heatherton was keeping a watchful eye over them both.

After Elsa brought out the pitchers of milk, Matty went back into the kitchen for a platter of hotcakes. She smiled at Elsa's mother.

"These sure smell good, ma'am."

"You don't have to call me that."

"Yes, ma'am."

Elsa's mother touched her shoulder. "You're a good girl, Matty Green."

Matty grinned broadly and backed out the swinging door to the dining hall. This wasn't terrible. In fact, it had almost been fun. She liked Elsa and her mother. Matty set the platter down near Miss Heatherton.

"Thank you, Miss Green."

"My pleasure, ma'am," Matty replied, nodding slightly. She caught Francesca looking at her and saw the tentative smile on her face. Matty smiled back then turned and went into the kitchen.

"This is the last of it," Elsa's mother said.

"Yes, ma'am." Matty took the two big bowls of applesauce. She leaned into the door, holding it open as Elsa passed her coming back into the kitchen. A moment later Elsa emerged, carrying two baskets of muffins.

They walked together between the two long tables. Matty heard Clarice whisper something as she ap-

40

proached, but she paid no attention to her. The applesauce bowls were heavy, and Matty had to concentrate. She set one bowl in front of Miss Heatherton, then started for the other end of the table.

Just as Matty got close, Clarice shot her foot out, smiling sweetly. Before Matty could react, she was falling. As she flailed her arms to try to catch her balance, applesauce was flung from the bowl, covering her own dress and spattering Elsa, who had turned to look. An instant later, Matty was facedown on the carpet. As she sat up, she heard the peals of laughter, and for a moment she wanted to pull Clarice from her chair. Then Miss Heatherton cleared her throat and the laughter died as she walked between the tables.

"Here, Matty," Elsa said, extending her small hand.

Matty stood up. All of the girls were giggling—even Francesca.

"Good heavens, are you girls all right?" Miss Heatherton asked, looking into their faces.

"Yes, ma'am," Matty said haltingly, her eyes on Clarice. "I'm just fine." Matty hesitated, still staring at Clarice. "I guess I just tripped, ma'am. I'll clean up the mess."

"That can always be done later. As long as you girls are all right. You two go wash up."

Matty and Elsa went back into the kitchen. While Elsa quickly explained to her mother what had happened, Matty got a rag and began wiping the applesauce from her dress. When she looked up, she saw Elsa smiling. "What?"

Elsa's eyes twinkled and she reached out to wipe a glob of applesauce from Matty's cheek. "You look pretty in applesauce."

Matty frowned, then grinned. "I think I like it. It's the new fashion from Paris, didn't you hear?" Matty dropped a curtsy. "The young lady was seen at the theater last night, wearing a full, flounced gown of applesauce." Both girls dissolved into laughter.

After a few seconds, Elsa's laughter died. "She hates you, Matty."

"You're not one of her favorites, either."

"She scares me."

"Don't let her. All you have to do is stand up to her."

"But I can't. If I did . . ."

Matty nodded. "I'm sorry, I forgot. It's not the same for you." She handed the rag to Elsa.

"Clarice was a troublemaker last year," Elsa said. "Nothing ever happened to her. She always makes it look like it's someone else's fault."

Matty met Elsa's eyes for a moment and she was sure they were thinking the same thing.

Chapter 4

Elsa stirred the bean soup, glancing uneasily at her mother.

"Stoke the fire, Elsa. Keep it hot."

Elsa found a slim log that would fit into the already full firebox. Sparks showered upward as she pushed it in. She looked once more at her mother and almost smiled. Her mother was finally gathering her dust rag and cleaning brushes.

"I'll be in Miss Heatherton's office. You make sure the soup doesn't burn."

"All right, Mama," Elsa said, absently stirring the thick soup. She waited for a minute or two, then hurried to the door, peeking through to make sure her mother had already gone up the stairs. Wiping her hands on her apron, she crossed the kitchen to the wood box. Kneeling, she reached underneath the kindling, reverently taking out the book.

Looking fearfully towards the dining hall, Elsa went

to the pastry table, opening the pantry door as she passed it. She had thought about it and this was the best place. If anyone came in, the open door would shield her long enough to give her a chance to hide the book on one of the shelves.

Keeping the primer on the towel, Elsa opened it. "*A*," she said softly, tracing the first letter of the alphabet. She knew a few letters. Once her brother had tried to teach her, but then had lost interest. Elsa felt a familiar stab of sadness. Karl had lost interest in everything except his tavern friends.

Elsa looked back at the book and smiled. Next to the letter *A* there was an apple, an ant and an ax, with words written underneath. One of the letters was like a cross tipped on its side. She turned to the next page. "*B*," she said aloud, as she looked at the pictures of a baby, a bumblebee and a book. "Book," she whispered.

"Elsa!"

Elsa closed the primer and flipped the towel back over it. Her mother's voice had come from the dining hall. Hands shaking, Elsa managed to tuck the book behind the flour bin and close the pantry door. By the time her mother came into the kitchen Elsa was back by the woodstove, stirring the soup. She pulled in an unsteady breath. "What is it, Mama?"

"I forgot to tell you to watch the muffins."

Using the pot rag, Elsa opened the oven door. "They're not brown yet."

Elsa's mother nodded. "Check them again in five minutes. Don't let them burn."

Elsa nodded and waited until her mother's footsteps had faded again. Then she took the book from the pantry and put it back beneath the kindling. Maybe she would

44

have to take it home. Then she would be able to look at it when her mother was asleep.

Matty walked down the dimly lit stairs and into the dining hall. She could hear the piano. The other girls were spending their free hour in the music room. Matty didn't want to join them, but she wasn't sleepy yet. She was tired of staring out the window at the river. It only made her feel lonelier.

She could see a thin sliver of light beneath the kitchen door. Without thinking about it, Matty pushed it open and went in. Elsa and her mother were still there.

"Do you need any help?"

"Matty?" Elsa's mother looked startled.

Matty scuffed her shoe on the spotless floor. "I just wanted to visit with you and Elsa."

"Didn't you get enough of that yesterday morning?"

"No, it's nice in the kitchen."

Elsa's mother walked over to Matty. "But you should be with the other girls."

Matty felt her eyes flood with tears. "I'd rather be in here with you and Elsa."

"Oh, Matty," Elsa's mother said, putting her arm around Matty's shoulders.

"I hate this school," Matty said, leaning against her.

"It'll just take some time, that's all," Elsa's mother said gently. "It's always hard to make friends when you go to a new place."

"I'm not like these girls, Mrs. Linstrom."

Elsa's mother put her hands firmly on Matty's shoulders and looked into her face. "Matty, it's just not acceptable for you to be in the kitchen with us."

Matty searched Mrs. Linstrom's soft blue eyes. "It

45

doesn't matter to you though, does it? You like me, don't you?''

Mrs. Linstrom smiled, reaching out to brush Matty's cheek. ''Yes, I like you, Matty.'' She straightened up, wiping her hands in a nervous gesture on the front of her apron. ''But you can't keep coming in here. As much as we like you, you belong with the other girls. Miss Heatherton wouldn't approve.''

''I don't care. This is my free hour. I can do what I please.'' Matty looked over at Elsa, noticing the worried expression on her face for the first time. She sighed. She wasn't the only one who might get into trouble. ''But if you think it will cause problems, Mrs. Linstrom, I won't come in anymore.''

Elsa's mother looked from Matty to Elsa. ''I don't suppose I can keep you out of the kitchen if you're hungry. After all, it is my duty to keep you well fed.''

Impulsively, Matty hugged her. ''Thank you, Mrs. Linstrom. Thank you.''

Mrs. Linstrom gently stepped back. ''I've just baked some raisin cookies. Are you hungry?''

''Yes, ma'am,'' she said eagerly. She exchanged a look with Elsa. They smiled at each other.

''Both of you sit down,'' Elsa's mother said, setting a plate of cookies in the middle of the pastry table.

''Is there milk in the icebox? I know where the glasses are,'' Matty said, turning.

Elsa's mother shook her head. ''Sit down, Matty.''

''Yes, ma'am,'' Matty said, reaching for a cookie. She took a large bite and chewed quickly.

Elsa's mother set two glasses of milk on the table. ''I have to blow out the lamps in the front rooms. Elsa, make sure you rinse those glasses.'' She turned and was gone.

Matty finished her cookie then leaned forward. ''I like your mother. She's nice.''

Elsa nodded, then her eyes narrowed as she glanced toward the door her mother had just gone out. ''Clarice pinched me today,'' she whispered.

Matty reached for another cookie. ''I can't believe she never gets in trouble.''

''Why can't she leave us alone?''

Matty shook her head. ''I wish we could put a spell on Clarice and make her disappear.'' Matty snapped her fingers. ''Like in a fairy tale.''

By the time Elsa's mother came back they were laughing, and the cookies were gone.

It was getting close to eight o'clock. Matty was reading a book of fairy tales she had borrowed from the music room. She kept glancing at the door. Every night this week Francesca had finished her lessons, then gone to one of her friends' rooms until almost bedtime. Last night Matty had seen her coming out of Clarice's room. As the tall clock at the top of the stairs began to strike eight, the door opened.

''What are you reading, Matty?'' Francesca asked as she came in. She began to unbutton her dress, her fingers flying over her bodice. Miss Heatherton always checked their rooms at ten past eight to make sure everyone was in bed.

Matty didn't answer. Francesca hadn't really talked to her for days. Why should she start tonight?

''Did you hear what I said, Matty?''

Matty looked at her over the top of the book. ''I heard you.''

47

"What's the matter with you?" Francesca was peeling down her stockings.

"Nothing." Matty refused to look up from the page as Francesca came over to her bed.

"Would you please talk to me?"

Matty laid the book on her chest. "Did you have fun with Clarice tonight?"

Francesca shrugged. "Four of us played some parlor games, that's all."

"I thought you said she wasn't your friend."

"I suppose she is, sort of. I like Annabelle better."

Matty raised the book again. She made a point of looking intently at the page.

Francesca sat on the edge of Matty's bed. "I thought we were friends, too."

"So did I. Why did you laugh at me and Elsa the morning I had to serve breakfast in the dining hall?"

"I didn't laugh."

"Yes, you did. You and all of the others." Matty pretended to read again.

There was a long silence, then Francesca spoke. "All right, I admit I laughed. But you did look funny."

Matty slammed the book shut and sat up. "Would you think it was funny if someone tripped you and you fell on your face in front of everybody? You'd die of embarrassment, Francesca."

"You were tripped?" Francesca asked, standing up.

"By Clarice. As if you didn't know."

Francesca went to their wardrobe. She took off her chemise and slipped on her nightgown before she turned to face Matty. "I didn't know that. Honestly I didn't."

"It doesn't matter."

Francesca sat down on the bed again. "Yes, it does,

48

Matty. You have to tell Miss Heatherton. Clarice should apologize to you."

"She'll never apologize," Matty said. "I just have to forget about it."

"I can't believe you aren't angry."·

"What can I do about it? I've already been in enough trouble."

Francesca tilted her head to one side. "I know why you don't want to tell Miss Heatherton. Clarice didn't do anything, did she? You just want to blame your accident on someone, and you don't like Clarice."

Matty narrowed her eyes. "I am not lying, Francesca. I'm not like Clarice." They heard Miss Heatherton's footsteps in the hall, and Francesca blew out the lamp. Matty lay in the darkness, her hands clenched into fists. She hated this place. She envied Elsa; at the end of the day, she got to go home with her mother.

Elsa stood with her back to the wood stove. Her mother had opened the grate to do her mending by the light of the fire. They had a lamp, but whale oil was too costly to use unless they had to. Elsa knew her mother would probably sew until bedtime. She had no other time for her chores.

Karl had been there when they'd gotten home from work, but then two of his friends had come by and he had gone out again. Elsa was starting to hate him. Whenever he argued with their mother he made her cry. Maybe he would just leave soon, as her father had.

Elsa stared into the fire. Her father had gone to the California gold fields when she was three years old. Her mother still had the letter, signed by his three partners, telling her that he had died in the wilderness there.

Elsa closed her eyes. Usually, while she waited for bedtime, she daydreamed. All her life she had imagined that she was a princess, living in a sparkling white castle. Lately though, her daydreams did no good. Instead of bringing her the peaceful, floating feeling they had when she was younger, they only made her sad. Elsa rubbed the back of her right hand, trying to work the lard her mother had put on it into her cracked skin.

Elsa looked longingly toward the bed she and her mother slept in. The coverlet was tattered but immaculately clean. Karl's cot was on the opposite wall, close to the table that served as their kitchen and parlor. Tonight's supper had been third-day bread and leftover stew from Miss Heatherton's. Their dishes were drying in the wooden rack; the table had been washed.

Elsa's mother tipped her old rocking chair forward. "Elsa? Put on a little wood."

Elsa took a piece of firewood and fit it into the stove. The fire flared up, lighting her mother's face. Elsa watched her sew. Every stitch was precise, careful. Her expression reminded Elsa of Miss Heatherton's when she was reading. "Have you ever wanted to know how to read, Mama?"

Her mother looked up at her. "Me? What in heavens for? It wouldn't make my job any easier."

"But you could come home and read the *Daily Missouri Republican*. You could find out things about the world from the newspaper."

"I have no interest in the world, Elsa. My interest lies only in doing a good day's work."

Elsa thought for a moment, trying to make her mother understand. "But Karl can read."

"Yes, for all the good it's done him. He spends his

time with gutter politicians. Crazy friends who want a war.''

Elsa sighed. "You could read me stories every night, Mama.''

"I tell you the stories my mother told me. I always have.''

Elsa knelt next to the old rocking chair. "I could learn to read, Mama. I could teach myself.''

"Don't be silly, Elsa. A person can't teach herself to read.''

"There are books that show the letters.''

Her mother looked up, laying her sewing in her lap. "And why are you talking about this?''

Elsa ran her fingers along the worn arm of the chair. "I don't know. I was just thinking if I ever had such a book, I could teach myself.''

"That's foolish. You dream far too much of things you can't have.''

"But, Mama—''

"There is no reason for you to learn how to read. Do you think Miss Heatherton cares whether I can read a book or the newspaper? No, she cares only that I am a good cook and a hard worker, and that is all you should be thinking about.''

Elsa fought back tears as she stood up. She started to go to bed but stopped and faced her mother. "I don't want the kind of life that you have, Mama.''

"Elsa!''

"I don't want to peel potatoes and be a servant.''

Elsa saw the pain in her mother's eyes but she didn't go to her. Instead she crossed the narrow room and got into bed. She lay on her side, crying silently to herself, ashamed that she had hurt her mother so.

*   *   *

Elsa apologized to her mother on the way to the academy the next morning. Her mother hugged her, then said no more—and Elsa was grateful. She did all of her chores more quickly than usual and then served breakfast. When the girls had left the dining hall, she helped clear the tables and wash the dishes. Then, sitting out on the little back porch, she rinsed and picked over the black-eyed peas they would have for dinner.

Only later, once her mother was upstairs changing the bed linens, did Elsa risk getting out the primer. She unwrapped it, laying the towel in the pantry. Holding the book tightly, she slipped out the back door and sat on the steps.

Sitting in the morning sunshine, she opened the book on her lap, turning the pages one by one. A feeling of magic washed over her as she looked at the bright colors and intricate letters. But this was better than magic, better than her little-girl daydreams. She traced each letter of the alphabet, trying to remember the shapes and wondering if she would ever learn their names.

"What are you doing?" Her mother's voice came from right behind her and Elsa jumped. She closed the book and held it to her chest, slowly standing, then turning to face her mother.

"What is that you are holding?"

Elsa was silent.

"Answer me."

Elsa grasped the book tightly. She didn't want to give it up. Her mother reached out and pried it from her hands. "Where did you get this?"

"I found it."

"Where?"

Elsa met her mother's angry eyes. "I found it behind the bookcase when I was dusting the music room."

"You stole a book from Miss Heatherton?"

"I didn't steal it, Mama. I found it. I was only going to borrow it."

"Oh, Elsa," her mother said, shaking her head. "You cannot take something just because you want to. That *is* stealing."

Her mother stood with her arms crossed. "You are going to put it back. We may be poor, but we are not thieves. You will tell Miss Heatherton what you have done."

"But what if she doesn't understand? Please, just let me put it back." Elsa watched as her mother closed her eyes for a moment, then finally nodded.

"All right. I want you to put it back where you found it. In the exact same place, do you understand me?"

"Yes, Mama."

Elsa took the book from her mother and walked slowly back into the kitchen, tears flooding her eyes.

"We'll practice our French again tomorrow, girls. *Au revoir,* and enjoy your morning break."

Matty stood up, keeping her eyes down. She was getting good at this. She preferred spending her break by herself and she had found that if she avoided eye contact with any of the girls, they left her alone.

Matty let the rest of the class stream past her, wishing that she had brought the book of fairy tales with her. Now she would have to go upstairs and get it. Maybe if she hurried she could avoid running into Clarice or Francesca in the hallway and get back down to the music room before it was too crowded.

The door to her room was open and she saw Francesca, bent over one of her trunks. When she straightened she had an armful of sheet music. Matty nodded but didn't speak. She picked up the book and turned to leave, her cotton skirts brushing Francesca's silk.

"Matty?"

Matty pretended that she hadn't heard and kept walking, her chin high. Francesca seemed to be puzzled by her coldness. What did she expect? Did she think that being laughed at and then called a liar was something so easily forgotten?

Matty went down the stairs quickly and strode across the dining hall. She just wanted to return this book and get another one without getting caught up in some silly conversation. Maybe she could find Elsa. She thought about going into the kitchen to look for her, then decided she'd better return the book first. She went through the door into the hall. As she turned toward the music room, she heard laughter—cold, sharp-edged laughter.

Matty stopped in front of the music room door. Clarice, Annabelle and Caroline were standing in a loose triangle around Elsa. Elsa's cheeks were flushed and she had tears in her eyes.

"What are you doing, Clarice?" Matty asked quietly.

Clarice looked up, meeting Matty's eyes. "It's none of your business, little Miss River Rat."

Matty pushed her way through the other girls and faced Clarice. Elsa looked scared. Matty knew she had to hold her own temper. No matter how angry she got, she had to remember that Elsa might get in trouble, too. Elsa began to cry quietly and Clarice mocked her, pretending to sob.

Francesca's voice startled Matty. "I don't think Miss Heatherton would approve of your treatment of her kitchen girl, Clarice. Maybe bullying people is acceptable etiquette at your home, but it's not in mine, or at this academy." She was standing in the doorway, the sheet music still in her hands.

Matty watched as Clarice hesitated, wrinkling her brow. "She's a thief," she said loudly. One by one, the other girls were leaving the room, brushing past Francesca. Juliana looked back once, but Sally pulled her along. Annabelle and Caroline hovered in the hallway, curious but ready to flee. No one wanted to get in trouble.

"Elsa would never steal anything," Matty said.

"What about this?" Clarice asked, holding out the primer.

Matty took the book from her. "We all borrow books from the shelves." She held up the book of fairy tales. "I came to return this and take another one."

"But you're a student here. That's different. She's a servant."

Elsa wiped at her eyes. "I only look at them sometimes, that's all."

"I'm sure you're not allowed to touch Miss Heatherton's books," Clarice said.

Francesca stepped forward. "Just leave her alone, Clarice."

"I don't have to, Miss Snooty. Just because all your dresses are silk and satin doesn't mean you can tell me what to do."

Matty watched Francesca. Her skin had gone pale and her eyes were flashing. "If you don't leave Elsa alone, I will go get Miss Heatherton right now."

Clarice glanced from Francesca to Matty. "This is stupid. What do I care what a servant does?" She turned, flouncing her skirt, and went out the door. After a moment Annabelle followed her up the hall, Caroline close on their heels.

Matty exchanged a quick, conspiratorial look with Francesca. "Thank you."

Francesca smiled. "Elsa, my name is Francesca. I don't believe we have ever met properly."

Elsa mumbled a polite answer and looked at them shyly. Matty turned to the bookcase. She slid the fairy tale book back into the shelf, then straightened up, uncertain. She held the primer out to Elsa. "Were you ready to put it back?"

Elsa shook her head. "I was trying to teach myself to read."

Matty looked at Francesca and got a little nod in response. "I'll help you," Matty said.

"So will I." Francesca laid her sheet music on the piano, then came back. She took the book from Matty and quickly paged through it. "This is a good book to start with."

Elsa wiped her eyes. "I want to learn. But I don't think my mother will allow it."

"If Miss Heatherton says it's all right, then your mother might let us," Matty said.

"Thank you both," Elsa said. "But I think I should talk to my mother first."

"Elsa!"

"I have to go now." Elsa handed the primer back to Matty. "Would you please put it on the shelf for me?" Her face was still pale.

Once she was gone Francesca turned to Matty and

shrugged. "You were right. Clarice *is* mean. She likes to cause trouble." She glanced at the piano. "Do you play?"

Matty shook her head.

"I can show you a fun song. It's simple." Petticoats rustling, Francesca walked to the piano and sat down. Matty looked around the room. She had never noticed how the sun streamed in this window. Everything in the room seemed to shine.

Chapter 5

The day after the incident in the music room, Matty and Francesca stood before Miss Heatherton's desk.

"Do you both know why I have called you in here? Clarice tells me that she caught Elsa stealing a book."

"It's not true," Matty blurted out. "Elsa wouldn't steal."

"Calm yourself and mind your manners, Miss Green." Miss Heatherton looked at Francesca. "I would like you to tell me what happened, Miss de Larmo."

Matty listened as Francesca told Miss Heatherton what had happened in the music room. When she was finished, Miss Heatherton turned her gaze to Matty. "Did everything happen as Miss de Larmo has stated?"

"Yes, ma'am. May I say something, Miss Heatherton?" Matty asked, careful to keep her voice calm and polite.

"Yes, you may."

"Elsa just wants to learn how to read. That's why

58

she was looking at the primer. I don't think there's anything wrong with that, ma'am. This is a school, after all.''

"But Elsa isn't a student, Miss Green.''

"Yes, ma'am. Does that mean she can't learn to read? Francesca and I can teach her during our free hour, when Elsa is finished with her chores.''

"Miss Green—''

"Please, ma'am, may I finish?''

Miss Heatherton nodded, her face unreadable. Matty took a deep breath. "I believe you said in class the other day that we, as young ladies, should find it in our hearts to be more charitable to people less fortunate than ourselves. Ma'am,'' she added quickly.

Miss Heatherton looked down, smoothing her lace cuff. After a moment she met Matty's eyes again. "Thank you for reminding me of my lecture, Miss Green.'' Miss Heatherton folded her hands on top of her desk. "I agree with you Matty. I think Elsa should learn to read. As long as you two keep up with your own studies and Elsa does not stint in her work, you may tutor her. You may use the dining hall, or your room might be quieter.''

Matty shot Francesca a joyous glance, then remembered how frightened Elsa had been to ask her mother. "Miss Heatherton?''

"Yes, Miss Green?''

"I'm not sure Elsa's mother will let her.''

"I'll speak to Mrs. Linstrom. Just make sure you two don't neglect your own lessons. Miss de Larmo, you may leave now. Miss Green, please remain for a moment.''

Matty felt her stomach tighten as Francesca went out

59

the door. It had been too good to be true. She was going to get into trouble after all.

Miss Heatherton was looking at her intently. "I just want you to know that I appreciate your restraint in the dining hall the other day, Miss Green. I know that Clarice tripped you. I am not unaware that she has a penchant for causing trouble. I have taken away some of her privileges and I am keeping my eye on her." Miss Heatherton cleared her throat. "In the meantime, you stay away from Clarice and her friends. You may go now."

"Yes, ma'am. Thank you, ma'am," Matty said hastily, hurrying from the room. She had barely closed the door to Miss Heatherton's office when Francesca appeared from around the corner.

"What happened? Did you get in trouble?"

"No," Matty said, shaking her head. "She thanked me for not losing my temper when Clarice tripped me." Matty looked into Francesca's face. "You told her, didn't you?"

"Yes."

Matty leaned close and whispered as they went down the hall toward their room. "Thank you. Miss Heatherton said she's going to keep her eye on Clarice."

"Good." Francesca opened the door and went in. She sat on the window seat.

Matty joined her. "Miss Heatherton was kind of nice to us, don't you think?"

"Yes, and now I'm sorry I called her an old prune-face in my journal."

"Francesca?" Matty said haltingly.

"Yes?"

"I'm glad you're going to help me teach Elsa to read. You'll like her."

Francesca fiddled with the silver buckle on her shoe. "Sometimes I think it would be nice to be a teacher, like Miss Heatherton."

Matty looked at Francesca, surprised.

Francesca laughed. "No one thinks I will do anything but marry well and keep a grand house. Especially my mother."

Matty turned to look out the window. She would never have thought about Elsa wanting to read, or Francesca wanting to be a teacher. She heard a steamboat whistle from somewhere downriver and smiled, thinking about her father. She would have to write him a letter soon and tell him he had been right. She had already made two friends here.

Elsa smiled as her mother stacked cookies and lemon tarts on a plate. "I read some words, today, Mama, and I wrote my name. It's only been two weeks. Francesca says I am a good student."

"I like it when you girls study in the dining hall. I like to watch you laughing together."

"You don't have to do this, Mama." Elsa pointed at the plate. Her mother smiled and shooed her out of the kitchen.

Elsa went back into the dining hall, carrying the plate. Matty had pushed the slate board and chalk to one side. Francesca was leaning back in her chair, laughing at something that Matty had said.

Elsa pulled out her chair and sat between them. As they began to eat the pastries, Francesca leaned forward. "I didn't want to tell you this before Elsa's lesson, because I knew we wouldn't get anything done once you knew.''

"What is it?" Matty demanded, grinning.

Elsa watched Francesca as she shook her head, one hand over her mouth. "You won't believe it."

"What?" Elsa said, reaching for a second cookie.

Francesca lowered her voice and glanced around the dining hall to make sure they were alone. "Clarice got into Miss Heatherton's cabinet and broke one of her favorite figurines."

"What was she doing? She knows no one's allowed to touch those," Matty said.

Elsa was astonished. "I'm not even allowed to dust them when I clean the music room."

Francesca glanced back toward the staircase. They were still alone. "Sally was there. She heard Annabelle telling someone that Clarice was going to take one of the figurines and put it in your desk, Matty."

"My desk?"

"Then she was going to tell Miss Heatherton that you stole it."

Elsa watched Matty carefully. Her eyes had narrowed and her face was pink.

Francesca dabbed at her mouth with a napkin, then continued. "Clarice tried to hide it in the folds of her dress but she dropped it. Sally said Miss Heatherton came into the room just as she had most of the pieces gathered up."

"Oh, my goodness," Elsa said, covering her mouth.

"What did Miss Heatherton do?" Matty asked.

"Sally said her face went white. I guess it was one of her favorites. She took the pieces from Clarice and ordered her to her office."

"It's about time," Matty said. She flipped her braid back over her shoulder. "Maybe now she will leave everyone alone."

Francesca nodded, but Elsa knew better. She picked up the slate and chalk and doodled. Clarice never seemed to be happy unless she was causing trouble.

Chapter 6

"*I* have a surprise this morning," Miss Heatherton announced from the front of the room.

Matty looked up, along with the rest of the girls.

"I think you will enjoy this," Miss Heatherton said, glancing at the watch pinned to her blouse. "We'll adjourn early this morning."

Matty caught Francesca's eye and smiled, raising her shoulders. What was this about?

"I want you all to go upstairs and get your bonnets, gloves, and parasols if you need them. If any of you has a little spending money, you might find you'll want it today. We'll meet on the front porch at exactly ten o'clock. You are dismissed."

Matty and Francesca went up the stairs to their room. All the girls were chattering noisily. As Francesca put her gloves on, Matty fidgeted with the strings of her crocheted purse. Francesca tucked a strand of Matty's hair back beneath her bonnet. "What do you think we're going to do today?"

Matty smiled. "I don't know."

"Are you going to bring any money with you?"

Matty nodded. "If we get to go into some shops, I already know what I want to buy."

"A new dress."

"No, silly, I don't have that much money. I want to buy a book for Elsa. One of those storybooks with pictures."

Francesca clapped her hands. "That's a wonderful idea."

Matty fished her white gloves out of the wardrobe drawer. Francesca was holding two bonnets, one of white dimity and the other of stiff, light blue linen. The blue linen had ribbon streamers. Matty knew it might take Francesca a long time to decide which to wear.

"Francesca, I'll meet you down on the front porch. I want to say good-bye to Elsa."

"All right," Francesca said absently, pulling a third bonnet out of her drawer.

Matty hurried out the door and flew down the hall and stairs, almost running into Miss Heatherton in the dining hall. "We still have five more minutes, Miss Green. You don't have to rush about so."

"I wanted to say good-bye to Elsa." Matty watched for a look of disapproval on Miss Heatherton's face, but it didn't come.

"While you're in there, why don't you get the basket of sugar cookies and coconut cakes Mrs. Linstrom is packing for us?"

"Yes, ma'am!" Matty scooted past Miss Heatherton and went straight into the kitchen. Elsa was at the washbasin. Her mother was setting the wicker basket on the pastry table.

65

Matty smiled when Elsa's mother looked at her. "It's a fine day for a walk, isn't it?"

"Yes, ma'am, it sure is," she said. "Miss Heatherton told me to come get the basket." She looked at Elsa. "And I wanted to say good-bye. I wish you could come."

"Me, too. Have a good time, Matty," Elsa said, her thin smile failing to hide her disappointment.

"I'll tell you all about it when we come back. I promise."

Elsa's mother turned, her hands full of cookies. "Don't you worry about Elsa. There's plenty to keep her busy right here."

Matty leaned close enough to whisper. "At least you won't have to worry about Clarice for a few hours."

Elsa nodded, giggling. "I know."

Matty looked at Mrs. Linstrom. "Do you think it would be all right if Elsa studied with us in our room tonight?"

"Oh, I don't know, Matty."

"Miss Heatherton said it's all right. Please?"

"Well," Elsa's mother said, looking at both girls, "I suppose it would be. We'll be here a little late, anyway. I have to mend tablecloths this evening."

"Thank you, Mrs. Linstrom."

"I'll carry the basket out, Mama," Elsa said.

Mrs. Linstrom nodded. "Don't be too long."

As they crossed the dining hall, Clarice and Annabelle were coming down the stairs.

"Well, if it isn't the river rat and the servant girl," Clarice said quietly. "How quaint they look together."

Matty stopped suddenly and faced Clarice.

"Don't, Matty." Elsa took her arm. "You'll only get into trouble."

Matty pointed at the green-glass vase at the foot of the stairs. "Be careful, Clarice. That's one of Miss Heatherton's favorites, too. And I'm sure its breakable." Matty watched as Clarice's cheeks darkened. She brushed past them, Annabelle close behind. Matty was pretty sure that this had been a battle of wits, and that she had just won. She looked at Elsa and they both smiled.

Miss Heatherton had had them choose walking partners. Matty walked beside Francesca. Behind them were Sally and Juliana, then the other pairs of girls. Miss Heatherton wore a broad-brimmed straw hat and strode along in front of them.

It was a beautiful fall day. About half the girls had brought parasols. Francesca had. And she had finally settled on a cream-colored cotton bonnet, set far back on her head to show off the *V* part in her hair.

Miss Heatherton stopped and pointed down Biddle Street toward the river, speaking in a clear, loud voice so that they all could hear. "You all know, of course, that our grand city of St. Louis is situated on the west bank of the Mississippi River. Front Street down by the river is also our wharf." Miss Heatherton gestured them forward. After another block or two, she stopped and faced them again. "Now, most of you were babies in 1849, but something terrible happened on the wharves that year. Can anyone tell us what it was?" Miss Heatherton looked at Matty when she put up her hand.

"My pa told me there was a big fire along the docks. It burned up about thirty paddle wheelers—and a lot of business houses down by the river. After that, they rebuilt the docks, and now the boats are farther apart so a fire couldn't spread like that again.''

Miss Heatherton thanked her for her answer, then walked on, leading them along the street, stopping once in a while to tell them something more about St. Louis. Matty felt the sun on her face and the cool breeze in her hair. As they crossed Fifteenth, she heard a steamboat whistle.

Once they were all safely across the street, Miss Heatherton spoke again. ''We all hear the steamboat whistles day and night. They carry tons of cargo every day on our wonderful Mississippi. It's quite amazing to think about. Snow that melts in Minnesota can be carried southward between the river's banks until alligators swim in it, down in Louisiana.''

Matty watched the girls' reactions. She wanted to tell them that she had seen alligators many times, whenever her father took on a cargo of cotton bales in Baton Rouge.

Matty turned to Francesca. ''This is kind of fun, don't you think?''

''My feet are sore.''

''We haven't been walking that long.''

Francesca frowned. ''I'm not used to walking. We always take one of the carriages.''

One of the carriages, Matty thought. She scowled. She'd like to take Francesca on a real walk, the kind her father loved, when they went all over New Orleans or Memphis on foot.

Miss Heatherton led them downhill toward the river. Matty glanced over at the brick building on her left and felt her throat tighten. It was the Girls' School at the

68

St. Louis Half Orphan Asylum. The name of the place had been enough to scare her when she was little. She had imagined being shut up in the cold building with other girls who didn't have both parents or good homes.

They crossed Fourth, Third, and Second Streets and reached Main. Then Miss Heatherton signaled them to stop again. "Stay with your partners. You may go into Dearson's Dry Goods, or the glassworks and china shop next to it."

Matty put up her hand. "May we go to Hampton's Bookstore? It's only a half block down."

Miss Heatherton nodded, then raised her voice again. "You may go to Hampton's Bookstore as well. No one is to cross the street or to go anywhere else. I will give you all one hour. Meet me back here precisely at twelve noon. Listen for the cathedral chimes."

Matty grabbed Francesca's hand. "Come on."

"Slow down, Matty."

"We don't have much time."

"I can't—"

Matty stopped and narrowed her eyes at Francesca. "I don't want to hear about your carriages, Francesca, or your sore feet. I just want to have fun today. Will you just try to keep up?"

Francesca nodded. "I'll try, Matty."

Matty led the way to Hampton's. She went inside, inhaling the familiar odor of leather and wood. She walked up to the smooth oak counter. "Hello, Mr. Hampton."

"Well, Matty Green. What're you doing in here without your father?"

"We're here with our school. We're looking for a

69

beginning reading book. Not a primer. We already have one of those.''

Mr. Hampton rubbed his chin for a moment then walked down one of the aisles of the bookstore. ''I think I have something here that might do,'' he said, pulling out a book and handing it to Matty.

Matty opened it and held it so Francesca could see. It was a volume of *Grimm's Fairy Tales,* and each page had a beautiful illustration. ''It's wonderful,'' Matty said, looking at Francesca.

''Elsa will love it.''

''This will do just fine, Mr. Hampton,'' Matty said, handing it back to him. ''How much will it be?''

''Well, being that it's leather bound and gilded, it's going to be a bit more expensive than most.''

Matty opened the strings to her purse and reached inside. ''How much?''

''Two dollars.''

Matty looked up, disappointed. That would take all of her money.

''But since you're such a good customer, I could make it a dollar-fifty.''

Matty looked at Francesca, then back at Mr. Hampton. ''Just a moment, please.''

''Yes, ma'am,'' Mr. Hampton said, going back to the counter.

Matty counted her money. She didn't have enough. Two dollars and ten cents wouldn't pay for the book and a gift for Miss Heatherton, too.

''Why don't we each pay half?'' Francesca said.

''You don't have to do that.''

''I have the money, Matty.'' Francesca handed seventy-five cents to Matty. "Can't you just imagine Elsa's face when we give the book to her?"

Matty squeezed Francesca's hand, then whirled to face the counter. "We'll buy it," she said pushing the money toward him.

"It's a handsome book," Mr. Hampton said, wrapping it in heavy brown paper. He tied the parcel with twine, snipping the ends with long bladed scissors.

When they left the bookstore, Matty made a beeline to the china shop. Francesca fell behind, but caught up at the door.

"Why do you want to go in here?"

"I want to buy Miss Heatherton another figurine."

Matty shrugged when Francesca arched her brows. "I like her."

Once they were inside, Matty walked carefully, her petticoats gathered in both hands. The shop was dim, but the glass sparkled anyway. Shelves along the walls held beautiful china dishes, crystal goblets, many colors of plates and bowls.

"May I help you, miss?" a well-dressed woman asked, a smile on her face.

"Yes, I'd like to buy a figurine for my teacher."

"I see. Do you have anything special in mind?"

Matty shook her head, glancing toward Francesca.

"Follow me, then." The woman guided them toward the back wall of the store. Shelves were lined with painted figurines. There were snarling tigers, tiny elephants, and horses in every pose and position. There were miniature glass children, laughing, crying, and rolling tiny hoops made out of wire.

"How much would you be wanting to spend, miss?"

Matty glanced down at her purse. "All I have is a dollar and thirty-five cents."

"The least expensive figurine I have sells for two dollars. These are all very fine. Imported from Europe." The woman took down a figurine and held it out for the girls to see. It depicted a smiling young girl with braids. She was wearing a simple dress and her hands were clasped behind her back.

"She reminds me of you, Matty. You have to get it." Francesca looked at the woman. "We'll take it."

"Francesca, I don't have enough money."

"I do. And I like Miss Heatherton, too."

Matty started to smile. "Are you sure?"

Francesca grinned at her. "Yes. I have never bought presents on my own like this before. It's fun." Francesca led the way to the front of the store, her silk skirts rustling. Matty followed, still smiling.

Chapter 7

Elsa could hear excited voices as the girls came through the gates. She set down her knife and went to the door, peeking out. Miss Heatherton was walking in front, her posture perfect, her broad-brimmed straw hat shielding her face from the sun. Elsa spotted Matty and Francesca, bringing up the rear, deep in talk.

"Elsa."

"Yes, Mama," she said, going back to the table and picking up her knife. "I'm almost done with the vegetables. I just have to peel the apples for the pies."

"Good girl."

"Miss Heatherton and the girls are back from their walk."

"Are they?" Elsa's mother asked absent-mindedly.

"I thought I should get the basket from them."

"I'm sure the girls are capable of bringing the basket to the kitchen."

"But—"

73

"Elsa, you must stop this."

"What, Mama?"

"This dreaming. You can't be like Matty or Francesca. You're not a student at this school. They are teaching you because it amuses them. They like you, Elsa, but you live in a shanty on Front Street. When you no longer amuse them they will forget about you. I don't want to see this break your heart." Elsa felt tears sting her eyes. Maybe it was the truth. Why would girls like Matty and Francesca care about her?

Elsa moped, doing her work mechanically. When she had finished all of the preparations for supper she sat down on the back stairs. She stared out at the oak trees. Two or three of them had limbs that grew out over the wall. It would be easy to climb up there and stand, looking out at the city. Elsa shook her head. She would never do anything like that. And she would never dress like a princess. She was going to end up like her mother, with red hands and no hope.

"Elsa."

"Yes, Mama," she replied without turning.

"Karl told me last night that he is leaving. He is going to head west."

Elsa spun around. "He's leaving?"

Her mother sighed. "I cannot stop him. And perhaps it will be for the best. He says the railroads are hiring."

Elsa turned back to her work, unsure what to say. In a way, it would be a relief to have Karl gone—but she would miss him, too. She thought about her father. He had never come back home. She shivered.

"Elsa," her mother said gently, "you have visitors."

Elsa glanced over her shoulder and saw Matty and Francesca. She hadn't heard them come into the kitchen.

74

Matty was shifting from foot to foot, barely able to conceal a grin. Elsa stood up.

"Look at the lovely flowers the girls brought me, Elsa," her mother said, proudly holding out a colorful bouquet.

"We have something for you, too, Elsa."

"For me?"

Matty handed her a brown paper package. "Here."

Elsa looked from her friends to her mother, then quickly tugged at the string that held the paper. It fell to the floor. She stared at the book for a moment, her eyes flooding with tears. She hugged it to her chest, then opened it, almost afraid to turn the thin, gold edged pages.

"It's fairy tales, Mama. See?" she said proudly, pointing out a picture of a princess dressed in a flowing white gown.

"It's a good one, Mrs. Linstrom," Matty said. "She can read the stories to you."

Elsa danced in a little circle until her mother stopped her.

"No, it's too much." Mrs. Linstrom gently took the book from her daughter's hands and held it out to Matty. "I thank you both, but Elsa can't accept your gift."

Elsa stared at her mother, aching to touch the book again, to try and read it. She managed a nod and mumbled a thank you, then turned and went back to the work table. She picked up her paring knife but stood motionless, trying not to cry.

"No," Matty said. "You can't do this."

Elsa looked up in time to see her mother's uncertainty. Matty was shaking her head. "I don't mean to be rude, Mrs. Linstrom, but this is something Francesca

75

and I want to do. It's our own money. Why would you take this gift away from Elsa and from us?"

Elsa saw anger cloud her mother's eyes. "Tell me why you want to do this, Matty. Is it because you feel sorry for Elsa?"

Matty shook her head. "Why would I? She's my friend."

Elsa wanted to hug Matty, but she was afraid of making her mother even angrier.

Elsa's mother looked past Matty. "What about you, Francesca? Do you feel the same way, or is this just charity?"

Francesca seemed startled, but she didn't hesitate. "Elsa is my friend. And a gift is not charity."

Elsa watched her mother's face soften, but still she said nothing for a long time. When her mother finally came to stand beside her, she gave Elsa a little nudge. "Go get your book, then, but don't forget we have work to do."

"Thank you, Mama," Elsa said, taking it from Matty. "This is so beautiful. Thank you both."

Matty smiled. "We'd better get back. Miss Heatherton is going to have an afternoon class on fine needlecraft," she said, rolling her eyes. Elsa almost laughed at the face she made.

"Good-bye," Francesca said.

Elsa watched her friends leave the kitchen, then turned to her mother. "Thank you for letting me keep the gift, Mama. You don't know how much it means to me."

"I think I'm beginning to, Elsa," her mother said. "But it frightens me." She smiled, then turned back to the pastry table.

*   *   *

Matty unwrapped the figurine and held it carefully in her hands. It was pretty, delicate. She ran her fingers over the smooth porcelain. She was sure Miss Heatherton would love it, and as soon as Francesca came back they were going to go give it to her together. Matty stared impatiently at the door. Francesca had gone to play for everyone in the music room, but she had promised to come back early. Matty stood up and paced the length of the room. It was getting late, and she didn't want to wait much longer. Abruptly she turned to the door.

Holding the figurine tightly in her hand, Matty went out and down the hall. As she passed the parlor palm, she hesitated, looking into the dining room below. Clarice and Annabelle were standing near the sideboard, talking. Clarice looked up. Clenching her teeth, Matty started down the stairs, trying to ignore her.

"Hello, Matty."

"Hello," Matty replied without looking at her.

Clarice stepped in front of her. Matty was forced to stop.

"What's that you're holding?"

"It's nothing."

"I just want to see it."

"Why?"

"Oh, come on, Matty. What is it?"

Matty looked at Clarice. She was smiling. So was Annabelle. Matty held up the figurine. "It's for Miss Heatherton."

"Is it?" Clarice bent forward, touching the shiny porcelain. "May I hold it, Matty?"

"No, I don't think that's a good idea."

77

"Miss Heatherton told me to be friendly, but you're not trying at all."

Matty heard the piano in the music room. If Francesca didn't come soon, they would have to wait until tomorrow to give Miss Heatherton her present. "I have to go, Clarice."

"Let me see it," Clarice said, reaching.

"Don't," Matty said, stumbling backward, but Clarice had already caught her wrist and was prying the figurine from her fingers. "Don't, Clarice, you'll break it," Matty pleaded, trying to free her hand. She felt the smooth porcelain slipping from her grasp and tried to hold it tighter, but it was already too late.

The figurine shattered the instant it hit the floor. Pieces as small as eyelashes skidded across the polished wood. Matty stood still, unable to say or do anything.

"I'm sorry, Matty."

Matty stared at Clarice, watching as the pale, freckle-faced girl began to smile. Matty began to tremble, so angry it scared her. "You are the meanest person I have ever known," she said, her throat so tight that it hurt to speak. She bent down and began to pick up the scattered pieces.

"What's the matter, Matty, are you afraid you won't be Miss Heatherton's pet, now?"

Matty froze. She slowly opened her hand and let the tiny chips of porcelain fall back to the floor. She straightened up, and glared at Clarice. Without thinking, she reached out and grabbed one of Clarice's pigtails. Clarice tried to wrench away but Matty held fast, pulling as hard as she could.

"Matty, let go, " Annabelle shrieked.

"What are you *doing?*" Clarice screamed. "Stop it,

Matty!'' Her high-pitched voice resounded in the dining hall, but Matty didn't loosen her grip.

"What in heaven's name is going on?" Miss Heatherton's voice came from behind them. Matty didn't turn. She knew she should let go of Clarice's hair now, but she just couldn't.

"Help me, Miss Heatherton. She's ripping my hair out," Clarice wailed.

"Let go this instant, Miss Green," Miss Heatherton ordered. Matty didn't look up, but Miss Heatherton's stern tone cut through her anger, and she obeyed.

"What is the matter with you two girls? Can't I ever leave you alone?"

"It wasn't my fault," Clarice sniffled, her face wet with tears.

Miss Heatherton took a deep breath. "Do you have anything to say for yourself, Miss Green?"

Matty didn't respond. She stared at the broken pieces of the figurine.

Miss Heatherton sighed. "Go sit at one of the tables. I will speak to you in a moment." Numb, Matty went to sit down. Everything had been perfect and she had been so excited. Now everything was awful. Matty raised her eyes to look at Clarice. She was sobbing as she told Miss Heatherton her version of what had happened. Looking past her, Matty suddenly saw Elsa standing just outside the kitchen door. She was pale.

Elsa felt terrible for Matty. She watched from the kitchen door as Clarice stood in front of Miss Heatherton, gesturing wildly, her voice shrill. Many of the girls were coming into the dining hall to see what was wrong. Clarice kept glancing around at her audience.

Elsa saw Francesca coming toward her, a worried, puzzled look on her face.

"What happened?"

Quickly Elsa explained. Francesca shook her head. "Why did I ever think Clarice was nice?"

Elsa didn't say anything. She continued listening intently as Clarice talked to Miss Heatherton. It was incredible. Clarice wasn't telling the truth about anything.

"I would like you all to go about your business now," Miss Heatherton said, suddenly looking up from Clarice. Reluctantly the girls went up the stairs. The dining hall began to clear out.

"I'm not leaving," Francesca whispered to Elsa.

"Neither am I." Elsa took a deep breath and stepped away from the kitchen door. She knew her mother wouldn't approve of what she was about to do, but it was the right thing.

"Miss Heatherton?" Elsa said hesitantly.

Miss Heatherton turned, an impatient look on her face. "What is it, Elsa?"

Elsa lifted her chin and spoke clearly. "She's lying." She pointed at Clarice. "I saw what happened."

"You did not," Clarice protested. "You didn't see anything."

"Please be still, Clarice," Miss Heatherton said, her voice short. "Tell me what happened, Elsa."

Elsa looked at Matty. She was sitting up straight now, watching. Elsa faced Miss Heatherton and told her what she had seen from the kitchen door.

Miss Heatherton thanked Elsa when she had finished. "You were there the entire time?"

"Yes ma'am," Elsa said. "Matty tried to ignore Clarice even after the figurine got broken. But Clarice kept saying mean things.''

"Did you see Matty take the figurine from my cabinet?''

Elsa shook her head. Francesca came forward. "It wasn't from your cabinet. Matty bought it for you in town today, Miss Heatherton. She wanted to give it to you to replace the one Clarice broke.''

"I see,'' Miss Heatherton said thoughtfully. She tucked a stray strand of hair back into her bun. "Go to my office, Clarice.''

"But Miss Heatherton—''

"Do not argue with me.'' Elsa noticed Annabelle on the staircase, still listening. Miss Heatherton followed her glance. "Annabelle, you go to your room.''

When the two girls had gone up the stairs, Miss Heatherton went to the table and sat down across from Matty. Elsa stayed next to Francesca, watching. Matty was still pale.

"Matty,'' Miss Heatherton said gently. Matty looked up. "Tell me what the figurine looked like.''

Matty shrugged and Elsa could barely hear her answer. "It doesn't matter now.''

"But it does. Please tell me,'' Miss Heatherton insisted. Francesca nudged Elsa and they smiled at each other.

"It was a girl,'' Matty said. "She had braids and she was smiling. I thought you'd like her because you teach girls.''

"I am sure I would have loved the piece, Matty.''

Elsa saw Matty hang her head again. "I'm sorry, Miss Heatherton. I didn't mean to do that to Clarice, it's just that she makes me so angry.''

"Well, we certainly do have a situation between the two of you, don't we?" Matty nodded. "Do you have any idea how we can resolve it?"

"I don't know, Miss Heatherton."

"Is it possible that you and Clarice could ever become friends?"

"No, ma'am," Matty said without hesitation.

"It seems you've made up your mind about her, then."

Matty took a deep breath. "Please don't ask me to be friends with Clarice. I can't do that."

"Clarice has some difficulty in her life, Matty."

Elsa watched as Matty shook her head and leaned forward. "I'm sorry for that, ma'am, but her life can't be harder than Elsa's, and she isn't mean to anybody."

Elsa blushed as she watched Miss Heatherton look out the window, then back at Matty. "I guess there's nothing else to say. You three run along, now."

Elsa turned to look at Francesca as Miss Heatherton spoke.

"There will be no punishment, Matty. However, I don't care what Clarice does in the future to make you angry; you don't attack her again. Sometimes it takes a better person to walk away."

Matty looked at the starburst of porcelain splinters still on the floor. She lifted her chin. "And sometimes a person has to stand up for herself, ma'am."

Francesca took in a quick little breath, but Elsa wasn't worried. Miss Heatherton would understand.

Miss Heatherton pressed the back of one hand against her lips for a moment and Elsa was almost sure she was trying not to laugh. But when she spoke her voice was serious. "I am certain you are right, Miss Green. It's getting late. Say good night to Elsa, and then you and Francesca run along to your room."

Matty stood and pushed in the chair.

"Matty?" Miss Heatherton said.

"Yes, ma'am."

"It doesn't matter that the piece is broken. The thought behind it will always be there."

Elsa watched as Matty turned toward them, her face lit with a smile.

Chapter 8

Elsa stood with her hands folded, listening as Miss Heatherton spoke to her mother. "As you know, Parents' Day will be a week from Saturday. It's so important that these parents see what a fine school we have. After all, we must compete with so many church schools. And everyone is watching their pennies now, even the wealthy."

"Yes, ma'am. Elsa and I will work hard to make sure it is a perfect day."

"I want to go over some things with you."

"Yes, ma'am."

Elsa watched Miss Heatherton as she looked down at her lists, muttering something to herself. Elsa almost smiled. Lately, Miss Heatherton didn't scare her as much as she used to. After what she had said to Matty, Elsa liked her even more.

"I want the best linen put on the tables," Miss Heatherton began. "We'll use the Stiegel water glasses and the silver meat platters I have put away in my quarters. We want to make it a special day, don't you think?'' She looked at Elsa's mother.

"Oh, yes, Miss Heatherton.''

"I'll want several fruit pies, four cakes, and two or three kinds of cookies. What about that wonderful lemon cheesecake you make, Lilia?''

"That sounds fine, ma'am.''

"Good. What were you thinking for the main course?''

Elsa's mother wiped her hands on her apron. "Last year we had baked ham with sweet potatoes, carrots, dilled beans, corn, and bread. We could do something different this year. Roast beef, perhaps.''

"That would be good, along with vegetables.'' Elsa's mother nodded as Miss Heatherton went on. "I'll want the meal set out on the tables and the desserts on the sideboard. We'll also serve coffee and tea for the parents, lemonade for the girls.''

"What time will the meal be, ma'am?''

Miss Heatherton looked out the window for a moment, then back. "Let's see. The parents will arrive at nine, they'll visit for an hour, we'll have our skits from ten to twelve. . . . So, let's say about one o'clock.''

"Yes, ma'am. Can you think of anything else, Miss Heatherton?''

"Actually, there is something else I need to speak with you about, Lilia.''

Elsa saw her mother's expression change, worry clouding her eyes. "What is it, ma'am, have I done something wrong?''

"Of course not, Lilia. Your work is outstanding, as always.'' Miss Heatherton folded her list, then looked up. "I want to speak with you about Elsa." Elsa tensed. Maybe Miss Heatherton was angry with her.

"If her lessons are interfering—"

Miss Heatherton held up her hand. "Let me finish, Lilia." Miss Heatherton smiled at Elsa. "Miss Green and Miss de Larmo have asked if Elsa may be in their Parents' Day skit. If you have no objection, I think it's a good idea."

Elsa held her breath and watched her mother frown. "But she is not a student here."

"Still, I think it's a good idea for the girls to do this together."

Elsa's mother was shaking her head. "I don't know, Miss Heatherton. We have so much work."

Elsa stood still, staring as Miss Heatherton turned to face her. "What do you think, Elsa? Can you manage both?"

"I think so, Miss Heatherton," Elsa said quickly, not daring to look at her mother. Her heart was racing with excitement.

"But, Elsa," her mother said, "when could you practice the skit? We don't finish until almost sunset, then we have to hurry home before dark."

Miss Heatherton walked over and put her hand on Lilia's shoulder. "I think there's a solution. If Elsa stayed here at night this week it would allow time for the girls to rehearse after they finish their schoolwork." Elsa could tell that her mother was upset. She would never let her stay over. "You know," Miss Heatherton went on thoughtfully, "I was proud of the way Elsa spoke up for Matty. Friendship like that isn't easy to find."

Elsa's mother nodded reluctantly. "If you think it's

a good idea, Miss Heatherton, I suppose it would be all right.''

"Good. It's settled, then." She looked at Elsa. "I don't want you girls wasting your time with needless foolishness.''

"Yes, ma'am. I won't disappoint you.''

Miss Heatherton nodded briskly. "Later today we'll make up the grocer's list for the Parents' Day supper, Lilia.'' Elsa waited until Miss Heatherton was gone, then she ran to hug her mother.

Elsa was so excited. Matty and Francesca would be coming downstairs at any minute, and she couldn't wait to tell them the news. Almost running back and forth between the kitchen and the dining hall, she carried a plate of cookies and three glasses of milk to their table. When she heard voices in the hall she smiled, but her smile quickly faded when she saw Clarice and Annabelle peek in, their wide skirts nearly filling the doorway.

"Oh, cookies," Clarice said, gathering her petticoats and walking to the table. "I'm starving." She reached for one of the cookies, but Elsa snatched the plate away.

"They aren't for you," she said firmly, meeting Clarice's eyes.

"What?''

Elsa didn't reply.

"What's the matter with you? I think you're forgetting your place.''

"The cookies aren't for you," Elsa repeated, still holding the plate.

Clarice looked at Annabelle. "Can you believe the kitchen girl is speaking to me this way?''

87

"No," Annabelle said, shaking her head.

"If you worked in my father's house, you'd be sent away for speaking to me so rudely."

"I don't work for your father. I work for Miss Heatherton."

Clarice narrowed her eyes. "I could make it so your mother loses her job. *Then* what would you do?"

Carefully Elsa set the plate on the table. She faced Clarice, standing so close that their skirts touched. She stared into Clarice's eyes, refusing to back down. "You couldn't do that," she said, her voice low.

Clarice stepped back. "We'll see if you feel that way after I've spoken to Miss Heatherton."

Elsa's hands were trembling and she clasped them behind her back so that Clarice wouldn't notice. "Miss Heatherton knows who tells the truth around here."

Clarice glanced at Annabelle, then nervously smoothed the skirt of her dress. "I didn't want a cookie, anyway. They aren't that good."

Elsa watched as Clarice and Annabelle went up the stairs. Her hands were still trembling. But she wasn't going to let a bully like Clarice push her around anymore. She sat down and opened the primer. By the time Matty and Francesca came in, she had practiced the whole alphabet.

Miss Heatherton had the girls working late. Tomorrow was Parents' Day. They were making swags out of red gingham cloth to hang along the stairway. So for a few more minutes, Elsa would be alone.

The room was quiet. Elsa kept looking out the window at the darkening sky. Never in all her dreams had she thought she would be sitting inside one of these

88

rooms, looking out. This was the second night she had spent at the school—and she wasn't as scared as she had been the night before. It had been strange, sleeping on the cot Miss Heatherton had let her use, but it had been wonderful, too, whispering until midnight with Matty and Francesca.

Elsa lay back on the window seat and closed her eyes. She and her mother had been scouring and scrubbing for three days, and there was still more to do. Some of St. Louis's most wealthy and influential people were coming, and Miss Heatherton wanted everything to be perfect.

The door banged open and Matty burst in. "Elsa!"

Francesca came in more slowly, a dreamy expression on her face. "If the swags and the streamers are going to be red, I think I will wear my white palentot jacket over my—"

"You are going to be playing a witch, Francesca, not a fairy princess," Matty said, shaking her head.

Elsa giggled at the expression on Francesca's face. She looked as though someone had given her lemon juice and told her it was honey. "A witch?" Francesca faced Matty, her hands on her hips. "What do you mean, a witch?"

Matty went to her night table and opened the drawer, pulling out some sheets of paper. Elsa could see that they were covered with Matty's slanted, sprawling hand-writing. She raised the papers with a flourish. "While you spent morning break doing your needlepoint and talking to Sally, I was hard at work on our skit."

Elsa stared at Matty. "I thought we were going to make it up together."

Matty frowned. "I figured someone had better get

89

started. All we did last night was talk." She lowered the papers and smiled at Elsa. "If you don't like it, we'll change it." The smile broadened into a grin. "But I think you will."

Francesca tilted her head. "Are you up to something, Matty?"

Elsa watched Matty settle herself on the edge of her bed. Matty cleared her throat and took a deep breath. Then she began to read.

"Clara was a miserable witch. She had no friends. The other witches tried to be nice to her, but she was always mean. Whenever a happy witch walked by, Clara tried to bully them. She made fun of their clothes, she stole their cookies and she broke their toys. So when the other witches went outside and played, Clara was always left alone. There were two witches Clara hated more than any of the rest: Elsie and Matilda. Clara had decided to put a spell on both of them, and no one could stop her—not even the good witch Heather—"

"The good witch Heather?" Francesca interrupted. "Matty, you've used all our names, except mine."

"We can use your name if you want—" Matty began.

"That's not what I mean," Francesca broke in again. "Anybody could figure out that you're talking about Clarice."

Elsa sat stiffly, unsure how to react. Matty was grinning again. "I want them to. Miss Heatherton said our skit should teach a lesson. She didn't say who the lesson was supposed to be for."

"I don't know, Matty," Francesca said, getting up

90

and walking over to the window. "It could get us all into a lot of trouble."

Matty shrugged. "You could at least listen to the rest of it."

"I think we should," Elsa said quietly. "Matty spent so much time on it." Elsa stared at the papers. It was hard to imagine being able to write down all those words. She was just learning to write her own name.

Matty picked up the skit and began reading again. As Elsa listened, she began to smile, then laughed out loud when Matty started barking like a dog and meowing like a cat. When Matty was finished Francesca sat still, her lips pressed together, her hands folded in her lap.

Matty slung the papers down on the bed. "You don't have to be mad at me, Francesca. We don't have to do my skit. We can pick one of the Greek myths if you want."

Elsa didn't want them to argue. Being in this room was special for her, and she didn't want a disagreement to spoil their time together. She stood up. "I think I should go down to the kitchen and get us something to eat before Miss Heatherton puts the lamps out. There are some raspberry tarts left. I put them way in the back of the cupboard so no one else would find them."

Francesca was shaking her head. "No, you stay here, Elsa. I'll go." Francesca stood up and straightened her skirt. "Try to talk some sense into Matty while I'm gone."

Francesca found the raspberry tarts back behind the clabbered milk, just as Elsa had said they would be. She wrapped them in a pastry cloth. Halfway to the kitchen door she decided she wanted milk, and went to the ice box and poured herself a glass. Careful to close the brass latch completely so the blocks of ice wouldn't melt before morning, she hurried out of the kitchen.

Quietly she went back upstairs. Most of the rooms were silent; it was almost eight o'clock. As she tiptoed closer to Clarice's room, she could see a little light escaping from beneath the door and she could hear voices. She grimaced as she stepped on a creaky part of the floor. The squeak resounded in the nearly silent hallway. The door opened suddenly and Clarice stood looking at her. Francesca would have gone on, but Clarice stepped out to block her way.

"Well, if it isn't Miss Snooty. Your room sounded like a barnyard a few minutes ago. Is all that noise part of your skit?"

"Maybe," Francesca said.

Clarice stared at the bundle in Francesca's hands. "What are you holding in that towel?"

"Food," Francesca said flatly.

"Miss Heatherton has told us it's against the rules to leave our rooms and go to the kitchen at night."

Francesca shrugged. "The lamps were still lit and I was hungry."

"Miss Heatherton doesn't like it when someone breaks the rules." Clarice wrapped one of her curls around her finger.

Francesca glared. "Do you think Miss Heatherton is going to punish me because I'm hungry?" She shook her head.

Clarice took a step backward, still staring. "I don't like you."

"You don't like anybody," Francesca said. "And almost no one likes you. Get out of my way, Clarice."

"No. You apologize first."

"What for?" Francesca balanced the milk glass carefully as she started to walk around Clarice.

"For saying no one likes me." Clarice reached out and grabbed at her wrist so quickly that Francesca had no time to react. Instinctively Francesca lurched back and the glass swung upward, splashing cold milk across her face and down the front of her dress.

For a long moment Francesca didn't move. Clarice was giggling, one hand over her mouth. Annabelle came to the door and peered out. Francesca lifted her chin, refusing to give them the satisfaction of seeing her lose her temper or cry. Still holding the raspberry tarts and her nearly empty milk glass, she stepped around Clarice and walked down the hall.

Just as Francesca got to the room, Matty opened the door. "What took you so—what happened?" Matty looked at the milk dripping from Francesca's chin.

Francesca went past her into the room. "Close the door."

"You've ruined your dress," Elsa said in disbelief. "Did you fall?"

Francesca walked to her desk, put the food down, then wiped the milk from her face with the washstand towel. Slowly, she turned to Matty and Elsa. "We'll do your skit, Matty."

Chapter 9

"**I** dare you," Matty said, leaning out of the window.

Elsa shook her head, smiling. It was just like Matty to come up with an idea like this. Since supper they had been rehearsing their skit and perfecting their animal sounds. Suddenly, Matty had decided they should sneak down the trellis and run across the lawns.

"I will not climb down there," Francesca said, crossing her arms. "It's silly."

Matty sat on the windowsill. "You'll climb down, won't you, Elsa? You told me before how you've always wanted to run on the grass.

Elsa hesitated. She knew if they got caught outside, Miss Heatherton would be really angry. Still . . . she walked toward the window. "If we just run around for a minute, then climb right back up, that should be all right."

"I think you are both foolish," Francesca said.

"We're going to have fun without you, then," Matty cajoled.

"Please come, Francesca," Elsa pleaded. If they argued too long, she was afraid she'd lose her courage.

"I'm afraid to climb. Aren't you?"

Elsa shook her head. "Sometimes when our roof leaks, I have to climb up and patch it."

Francesca sighed, giving in. "I suppose if you can do that, I can climb down this silly old trellis."

"You can, Francesca," Matty said, "we'll help you. I'll go first."

Elsa stood at the window with Francesca, watching Matty scramble down the trellis. She turned to Francesca. "You should probably take off most of your petticoats. They might get caught on something."

Francesca carefully slid out of her hoops and stiff crinolines, then stood by the window, taking in a deep breath. She leaned out. "If I fall and break my neck, I will never forgive you, Matty Green."

"You are not going to break your neck. All you have to do is listen to me and Elsa." Matty's voice was a rasping whisper that sounded too loud in the peaceful evening air.

Trembling with excitement, Elsa touched Francesca's shoulder. "Do you want me to go before or after you?"

"Before. I'll watch you."

Elsa nodded and took a deep breath. She sat on the windowsill, then turned over, sliding downward to find a foothold. Hitching up her skirts, she looked down at Matty, who was grinning up at her. The night air was soft against her face as she made her way to the bottom of the trellis. She stood next to Matty in the grass. "Come on, Francesca. Just do what I did."

"Oh . . ."

Elsa heard Francesca mutter to herself as she edged onto the window ledge.

"I hope she can do it," Matty whispered.

"Me, too," Elsa breathed, still watching as Francesca turned to start down the trellis. Even without her hoops and petticoats, her skirt was so full that the silk billowed out from her legs.

"It's almost like a ladder," Matty called softly. "Just come down slowly."

Elsa saw Francesca hesitate, then slip. She hung from the window sill, her arms straight, her legs kicking wildly. Elsa started forward, bumping shoulders with Matty. Matty stepped aside. "Hurry up. She's going to fall, Elsa."

Elsa went up the trellis as fast as she could. When she was just beneath Francesca, she started talking, keeping her voice as steady as she could. "Hold still. I'll help you find a foothold." Francesca stopped kicking and Elsa guided her feet onto the wood, one at a time. Once Francesca had calmed down, she began to make her own way. Elsa leaned sideways, letting her go past.

A moment later Francesca stood at the bottom, half smiling, a look of breathless astonishment on her face. "I can't believe I did that."

"You did fine," Elsa said, hopping down to the ground.

Matty was smiling, too, as she knelt to take off her shoes and stockings. "I'm glad you decided to come, Francesca."

Leaving them at the base of the honeysuckle vine, Matty began to run. Elsa watched her race across the lawn, curving back toward her friends in a long arc.

96

"What is she *doing?*" Francesca demanded. Elsa didn't answer. She slipped off her own shoes and rolled her stockings down. She walked a few steps on the cool, damp grass, feeling almost dizzy. The night was like magic. She lifted her skirts and ran. Matty caught her hand as she passed and they whirled in a giggling circle in the moonlight. Then they raced back across the lawn, straight at Francesca.

Before Francesca could refuse, they each took one of her hands and pulled her with them. They zigzagged across the grass, Elsa taking the lead, their hands clasped, pulling each other along. Stumbling as they began to laugh, the three girls stopped, covering their mouths and glancing back at the school.

"I have never had friends before," Elsa whispered, taking Matty's hand so that they formed a circle.

"Neither have I," Francesca admitted. "But we have each other, now."

"Yes. We are like the Three Musketeers," Matty said.

Elsa was puzzled. "Who?"

"They were soldiers who fought together during the French Revolution," Francesca answered. "But we aren't like them. We need a name of our own."

Elsa looked up at the high wall that surrounded the school. Moonlight silvered the top. "I wish we could get up there." She pointed.

Matty followed her gesture. "We could, I bet. Some of the trees grow pretty close to it."

Elsa turned. It could work, she thought. She scanned the nearby oaks, squinting to see in the darkness.

"No," Francesca said emphatically. "You aren't going to do that." Then she gasped. "Miss Heatherton is in the dining hall, turning out the gas lamps. We have to get back.''

Francesca ran, but Matty and Elsa quickly overtook her. While they gathered up their shoes and rumpled stockings, Francesca started up the trellis. Elsa climbed after her, with Matty close behind.

When Miss Heatherton opened the door their lamp was out and they all three seemed to be sleeping peacefully. The moment she closed it, Matty began to giggle. Matty got up from her bed and finished undressing. Francesca hung her damp dress over her desk chair. Shivering, Elsa changed into her nightgown. Back in bed, they practiced their skit one more time, whispering the lines they would say in unison. For a long time afterward Elsa lay awake, looking out the window at the stars.

Elsa thought everything looked beautiful. She smoothed the skirt of the dress Matty had loaned her. The parents would be arriving in a few hours. Miss Heatherton walked slowly around the dining hall. Elsa stood next to her mother as Miss Heatherton examined each place setting. The napkins were bleached to snowy whiteness, the silver polished until it shone like mirrors. Miss Heatherton stood back to evaluate the effect of the centerpieces. The Waterford cut glass bowls were filled with gold and red autumn leaves; dried barley was arranged in fans around their bases. Miss Heatherton even checked the chairs to make sure they were in perfectly straight lines along the two long tables. Then, she walked to the sideboard.

Elsa knew that Miss Heatherton would be impressed with what her mother had done. She had baked six fruit pies (two each of apple, peach and serviceberry), assorted delicate little cookies, and four lemon cheesecakes on green-glass plates.

"Well, Lilia," Miss Heatherton said to Elsa's mother, "I must say you've outdone yourself this time. If I'm not careful, one of the other schools is going to try to steal you away from me."

Elsa smiled up at her mother, but her mother remained somber. "Thank you, Miss Heatherton. Dinner is coming along nicely."

"I'm sure it is," Miss Heatherton replied. "Everything looks wonderful. You are going to watch Elsa in her skit, aren't you?"

"I don't know. There's so much to do."

"Please, Mama?" Elsa said quickly.

"Lilia, the kitchen won't burn down if you leave it for a few minutes."

"Yes, ma'am," Elsa's mother said, smiling.

"Well, thank you, Lilia. It really does look lovely."

"Thank you, Miss Heatherton," Elsa's mother replied.

"Elsa, if you're done helping your mother, you should go to the music room," Miss Heatherton said. "Parents will be arriving soon."

Elsa looked at her mother. "Mama?"

"You go, I'm almost finished here. I'll be in to watch you."

"Yes, ma'am. Thank you, ma'am," Elsa said, hurrying into the kitchen. She quickly untied her apron, threw it on the pastry table, then went out the side door into the hallway. Again she ran her hands down the skirt of the blue silk dress that Matty had loaned her and looked down at her shiny shoes, also Matty's. The

99

night before, Francesca had curled her hair around twisted strips of rag, and now it lay softly on her shoulders. She felt prettier than she ever had in her whole life.

Squaring her shoulders, Elsa walked into the music room. Neat rows of chairs had been set in front of the podium. Groups of girls were standing around, saying their lines, or acting out scenes. Matty and Francesca were by the windows. Elsa went to them.

"You look so pretty, Elsa," Matty said.

"Yes, you do," Francesca agreed. "Your hair is as shiny as gold."

Elsa blushed. "Thank you for loaning me the dress and shoes, Matty. I'll make sure nothing happens to them."

"Those shoes are too tight for me, anyway. They fit you, you should keep them."

Elsa shook her head. "No, I couldn't—"

"We should be practicing, shouldn't we?" Matty interrupted her, smiling.

"It will be starting pretty soon," Francesca agreed.

"All right." Elsa took her sheets from Matty. She had practiced her part over and over. She made a frog sound, very softly. Matty looked toward the door. She grinned broadly. "There's my father." Elsa watched as Matty ran across the room. Her father was a tall, handsome man with dark hair and an easy smile. He hugged Matty for a long time.

"I wonder where *my* parents are," Francesca said. She kept looking anxiously toward the door every few seconds.

"They'll be here soon," Elsa said. "Don't worry." She watched as Matty and her father came toward them.

She smoothed the beautiful blue skirt and hoped he wouldn't mind that Matty had loaned her a dress.

"Pa, this is Elsa Linstrom and Francesca de Larmo," Matty said proudly.

Ben Green grinned broadly. "Ladies, I'm very pleased to meet you. I hoped that Matty would find friends here."

"Pleased to meet you, sir," Elsa said, curtsying.

"I'm happy to meet you, Mr. Green," Francesca said.

"I'm acquainted with your father, Francesca. He's contracted with me many times to take consignments downriver." Ben Green looked around the room. "Is he here?"

Francesca glanced toward the door once more. "No, but he and my mother should be arriving at any moment."

Miss Heatherton's voice rose above the murmur of voices in the music room. "It's time for the parents to take their seats. Let's begin our program. Girls, I'd like you all to come into the dining hall with me. Quickly now." She clapped her hands lightly.

"Where are my parents?" Francesca whispered, and Elsa could see how upset she was. Elsa took her arm and led her toward the hallway. Matty joined them.

"Miss De Larmo, I need to speak to you," Miss Heatherton said as they walked into the dining hall. Elsa watched Francesca's face as Miss Heatherton spoke to her. She leaned close to Matty. "I think it's something about her parents." Elsa and Matty waited impatiently until Francesca returned. She tried to act as if nothing was wrong, but she couldn't hide the tears in her eyes.

"What happened?" Elsa asked.

Francesca bit her lower lip. "My parents aren't coming. The messenger told Miss Heatherton that they have an important social engagement to attend today.''

Matty took Francesca's hand. "I'm sorry."

"So am I," Elsa said.

Francesca shook her head. "They promised this time. I can't believe they're not coming." Francesca tried to smile and brushed the tears from her eyes. She took a deep breath.

"Girls, I want the first skit ready to go," Miss Heatherton said. Sally's group gathered around Miss Heatherton, then followed her back across the hall. Elsa could hear Miss Heatherton's voice as she welcomed the parents and introduced the first performers. A scattering of applause ended as Sally began to speak the first line of their skit.

Chapter 10

Elsa's heart was pounding. She knew all of her lines, but it was going to be very different saying them in front of all these people than it had been with Matty and Francesca in their room. She could only hope the skit wouldn't make Miss Heatherton angry. It had seemed so perfect as they rehearsed it; Clarice's part was entirely innocent. None of the parents would know anything.

As Miss Heatherton introduced them, Elsa glanced at Francesca. She looked nervous, but she also looked sad. It was awful that her parents hadn't come. Elsa saw her own mother come in and stand by the door, leaning against the wall. She smiled, and Elsa smiled back. Elsa crossed her fingers. If Miss Heatherton didn't get angry, this was going be fun.

At Miss Heatherton's gesture, Elsa walked forward with Matty and Francesca and they stood in a line with Matty in the center, just behind the podium.

Matty looked out at the audience. "We're going to perform a skit called *The Little Witch Who Learned How To Be Nice*. Matty paused while the audience reacted. Some of the parents laughed a little and the girls clapped. Elsa saw Matty's father beaming up at them.

"We're going to need one person from the audience to help us," Matty said as the murmuring died down. Elsa watched as several parents raised their hands to volunteer, as did three or four of the girls. Matty stepped around the podium and walked down the center aisle. She kept looking right and left, pretending to make up her mind. "Clarice Laraby," she said loudly. "You'll be perfect." Clarice had not raised her hand and Elsa heard her gasp when Matty named her.

Matty leaned into the row of chairs and tugged at Clarice's arm. Elsa couldn't hear what Clarice was whispering, but it was obvious that she didn't want to come. Matty answered Clarice loudly enough for all to hear. "It's a fun part, Clarice. You play the good witch, Heather. All you have to do is read a little speech. Come on, everyone's waiting." Elsa watched Matty escort Clarice to the podium.

Miss Heatherton had gone to join Elsa's mother by the door. Elsa glanced at them. Both their smiles had faded. Elsa swallowed hard. There was no turning back now. Matty handed Clarice her part and was positioning her to one side, seating her in one of the spare chairs. Then Matty came back to the middle of the room and nodded at Elsa and Francesca. They began to recite the introduction to their skit in unison.

"Clara was a miserable witch. She had no friends. The other witches tried to be nice to her, but she was

104

always mean. Whenever a happy witch walked by, Clara made fun of her clothes, she stole her cookies and broke her toys. So when the other witches went outside and played, Clara was always left alone. One day she walked to the edge of the forest. There she saw two happy witches playing together.''

They finished reciting exactly together and Matty smiled as she stepped off to one side. Matty kept narrating while Elsa and Francesca went to the center of the room in front of the podium. They pretended to be the witches, playing happily at ring-around-a-rosy.

''The happy witches were named Elsie and Matilda. They were the best of friends. They helped each other if one of them got into trouble.''

Here, Elsa pretended to fall down and Francesca helped her up, comforting her. Elsa glanced at Miss Heatherton. It was impossible to tell what she was thinking. As Matty continued to read, Clarice stood glaring.

''Elsie and Matilda shared happy times and sad times.''

Elsa and Francesca pretended to laugh, then cry together. The audience chuckled appreciatively as Francesca pulled a handkerchief from her pocket and offered it gallantly to Elsa, who loudly blew her nose. Matty continued reciting to the audience.

''As Clara watched these two friends, she became angrier and angrier.''

Then she walked out from behind the podium and assumed the character of Clara as she walked. By the time she had taken three steps, her expression had changed into a scowl. She had narrowed her eyes and when she spoke, her voice was shrill.

"I cast a spell on you both! You will become warty toads, too ugly for anyone to love!"

As Matty said her line, Elsa and Francesca fell to their knees. They had practiced making frog sounds all week, and now it paid off. The audience giggled and clapped. Matty waited until they had all fallen silent before she spoke her next line.

"Why don't you hop apart? How can you like each other? You are both incredibly ugly and warty."

Elsa and Francesca said in unison,

"We are friends. We are friends forever. It makes no difference to us that we are ugly."

They made their frog noises again. Elsa tried to see Miss Heatherton's face, but from her frog position on the floor she couldn't see much. She could see Clarice though, if she looked back over her shoulder. Clarice was not laughing.

"I will turn one of you into a dog and the other one into a cat."

Matty drew her hands up high as though she were a

witch casting a spell. Elsa and Francesca stood up side by side. Francesca barked and Elsa meowed like a cat. But then they leaned against each other, resting their heads on each other's shoulders.

"Friends don't have to be alike. They can love and understand each other anyway."

Elsa faltered on the last part of the line, but Francesca waited for her to catch up before she went on.

"Friends are nice to each other."

Elsa stole another look at Miss Heatherton as the skit went on. She thought she saw a little smile on her lips, but it was hard to tell. Matty's next lines changed Elsa and Francesca into a tree and a stone. The tree grew closely about her friend and the stone helped hold the tree safe from storm winds.

Matty acted the part of Clara with great feeling. She shrieked her frustration when none of her spells worked to separate the happy witches. Their friendship endured everything.

When it was time for Clarice's part, Matty signaled to her. Clarice stepped forward reluctantly, raising the paper Matty had given her.

"I am the good witch Heather."

Clarice read, then looked over the top of the paper to glare at Matty before she continued.

107

"I will tell you how to have friends of your own so that you are not so lonely and unhappy, Clara."

Matty looked up as though Clarice's voice had startled her, playing her part as Clarice continued to read. She tilted her head, acting as though she were listening intently.

"If you are nice to people, if you try to be a good friend, then you shall have friends of your own. You could begin by apologizing to poor Elsie and Matilda for all the trouble you have caused them, Clara."

Clarice frowned while Matty recited an elaborate apology to Elsa and Francesca. They forgave her, asking if she wanted to be their friend. Matty looked back at Clarice, gesturing for her to read the last few lines of the good witch, Heather. Clarice frowned, but began reading.

"Try to remember this all of your life, Clara. Kindness makes friends, meanness makes loneliness."

Matty bowed along with Francesca and Elsa as the audience clapped. Clarice bowed, too, after a second's pause. Then she laid down the paper and went to the back of the room to rejoin Annabelle. The audience continued applauding as Matty, Francesca and Elsa walked down the aisle to take their seats. Once more, Elsa tried to read Miss Heatherton's face, but could not. Her mother smiled at her, but it was a nervous, tentative smile. Elsa wanted to tell her not to worry. If Miss

Heatherton punished them, it would only affect Elsa—not her mother's job. Miss Heatherton was fair.

Elsa felt her stomach tighten as Miss Heatherton went to the front of the room, but once she was behind the podium, she smiled. "Thank you, girls. That was very entertaining." Without another word about their skit, she introduced the next group of girls. Elsa exhaled, leaning back in her seat. Maybe everything would be fine. Maybe Clarice would think about what they had said.

After the parents finished the meal and the tables had been cleared, Elsa took off her apron. She carefully checked the dress Matty had loaned her. There were no stains on it. Miss Heatherton saw her come into the dining hall and gestured. Elsa hesitated, afraid she was about to get a lecture for the skit. But Miss Heatherton was smiling.

"Your friends are out on the lawn with the rest of our guests. Be especially kind to Francesca. I think she is terribly upset about her parents not coming."

Elsa nodded. "I will, Miss Heatherton." She went out the front doors and across the porch. As she stepped onto the lawn, joining the swirl of color and talk, she remembered how they had run across the grass barefoot and it made her smile.

"Elsa?" It was Matty, sitting on the seat of a bright yellow carriage. Beside her was a negro man dressed in a dark suit and a snow white shirt with lace cuffs. Francesca was listening to something Matty's father was saying. As Elsa got closer, Matty called out again. "Hurry up, Elsa. This is Lafayette."

Elsa picked up her petticoats and ran the last few

109

steps, so that Matty wouldn't shout again. A number of people had turned to look.

"You're missing the best part," Matty grinned. "Lafayette is doing card tricks."

Elsa watched Lafayette's slow smile. "I was about finished, Miss Matty." He had a wonderful voice, deep and musical, with an accent Elsa had never heard before.

"Lafayette, do the last one over," Matty pleaded. "At least do one for Elsa. Please."

Lafayette winked at Elsa. "This child thinks that the seasons would turn around if she wanted them to."

Elsa smiled. Lafayette's accent made everything he said sound like one of the poems Francesca had read to her.

"Francesca wants you to do another trick, too," Matty insisted, poking Francesca until she giggled and nodded.

Matty's father grinned. "You may as well, Lafayette. There will be no peace otherwise."

"I will do a very special trick," Lafayette announced. "And then no more. I doubt if your Miss Heatherton has much use for riverboat gamblers who carry cards in their suit pockets." He paused and made a great show of looking around furtively. Then he nodded. "For the moment we are safe. I see her talking to the good witch's parents."

Elsa stared. "I told him," Matty admitted.

Matty's father laughed. "She told us both. I hope you don't mind. We won't let the secret go any further." Elsa nodded slowly. Matty's father smiled once more. His teeth were white and even.

"Now, *cheri,* we begin," Lafayette said. Using the carriage seat as a table, he laid the deck of cards down and flicked it with a fingertip. The cards slid, spreading apart as evenly as pickets in a fence. Lafayette flicked them again and the cards obediently reformed themselves into a solid deck. With one hand he shuffled, then cut the deck. The cards fell neatly back onto the stack in his palm.

Still using only one hand, Lafayette fanned the cards into a rosette, then whirled it closed. He shuffled a second time. "And now, *cheri,* you may choose a single card." He fanned the deck again and proffered it to Francesca.

She started to choose, then hesitated. "Let Elsa. She hasn't had a chance yet."

Lafayette gestured grandly, fanning the deck once more. He lowered the deck so that Elsa could see. Elsa looked questioningly at Matty. She nodded. "Just pick one. Any one you want. Then look at it."

Elsa raised her hand and indicated a card near the center of the fan. Lafayette let her pull the card free.

"Show it to the other young ladies. Not to me."

Elsa held the card carefully so that Lafayette couldn't see, showing Matty and Francesca. It was the three of hearts. Lafayette held the deck out toward Elsa. "Now, I want you to put that card back. Don't let me see it."

Elsa held her breath as she pushed the card into the deck. "All right."

"Good," Lafayette said, shuffling. The cards seemed to come alive in his hands. They leaped up, then arched and rearranged themselves, always falling back into a neat pile. Lafayette looked at Elsa and slowly fanned the deck once more, face up this time.

Elsa watched as he ran his finger over each card,

hesitating on the ace of spades. She glanced at Matty and saw the look of disappointment on her face.

Lafayette picked up the ace of spades. "This isn't the card," he said in his smooth voice. "I just wanted to give you ladies a scare." His eyes were twinkling. Francesca giggled and Matty's father laughed aloud.

Matty tapped Lafayette on the shoulder. "No more scares."

Elsa watched as Lafayette looked at all of the cards a moment longer. Then he reached down and pulled out the three of hearts.

"What other card could it be?" he asked, holding it up.

"I knew you could do it, Lafayette." Matty hugged him.

"How did you do that?" Francesca asked.

"It's like magic," Elsa said. She looked back down at the deck. How could he have known which one she'd picked?

"This is a special card, you know," Lafayette said, flipping the three of hearts over, turning it between two fingers so that the hearts flashed, then disappeared. "Look. There are three hearts." He gestured at each one of the girls. "And three friends." Lafayette grinned. "You are the three of hearts."

Elsa smiled at Matty and Francesca and then looked back at Lafayette. He was leaning forward, offering her the card. "You ladies should keep this. It will bring you luck."

Elsa took the card and held it tightly, staring into Lafayette's dark, handsome face. She would keep it forever.

112

Chapter 11

After the parents had left and the school had quieted down for the evening Elsa was finally alone with Matty and Francesca. Elsa shared the window seat with Francesca. Matty sat on her bed. They were all in their heavy flannel nightgowns, their dresses carefully hung in the wardrobe.

"I'm so glad your mother let you stay one more night," Matty said.

Elsa grinned. "I am, too. Did Miss Heatherton say anything to you about the skit?"

Francesca shook her head.

Matty laughed. "She told me the battle of wits was over and it looked as though I had won."

Elsa giggled. "Clarice was almost nice to me this evening."

Francesca leaned forward, her eyes wide. "Really? You mean she walked past without insulting you?"

Elsa nodded. "And she even said please when she asked me to bring more gravy at supper."

Matty clapped her hands. "Did you see the look on her face when she had to read her lines?" Matty bounced to her feet and postured. "May I introduce the good witch, Heather?"

Elsa laughed, then glanced out the window. The night was clear and warm. The moonlight made murky shadows beneath the oak trees. "Let's go out on the grass." Elsa turned and slid the window up. She might never have another chance. "Please? Just for a minute or two."

Francesca groaned, but she stood up. Matty was nodding eagerly. Elsa went down first. It was easier barefoot, and she wasn't as scared. This time Francesca didn't need help. By the time Matty reached the bottom of the trellis, Elsa and Francesca had already walked out onto the lawn. Elsa was still leading the way. For some reason, she didn't feel like running tonight. Instead, she just wanted to breathe in the crisp, fresh air.

"I wish we could see the river," Matty said, then she pointed. "From up there we could."

Francesca groaned again. "We could also fall on our heads."

"The wall is wide and flat, Francesca. If you aren't falling down here, you won't once you're up there. Don't worry."

Francesca laughed. "I don't have to worry. We can't get up there."

Matty caught Elsa's eye and they both turned to look at the oaks that grew at intervals along the wall. "That one?" Matty pointed.

Elsa began to walk. As she got closer, she nodded. "I think we could do it." She glanced back at the lighted windows. "But we can't stay too long."

"We won't," Matty promised, starting up the tree. Elsa followed. It was an easy climb. The trunk slanted. They paused, waiting for Francesca.

She stood beneath the tree, watching them. "Come on, Francesca. You can do it," Elsa urged. Francesca made an unhappy little sound, but she started to climb. Wobbling and shivering, she followed them.

Matty and Elsa climbed to the wide, solid branch that grew across the lawn to the wall. Then, one at a time, they walked it, holding their arms out for balance. Elsa's heart thudded against her ribs, but she forced herself to keep going.

Francesca hesitated. Ignoring her own trembling knees, Elsa argued with her. "You're going to be so sorry you missed this. You just have to come with us."

With both her friends encouraging her, Francesca finally managed to sit down, then scoot along the oak branch. Matty and Elsa took her hands and helped her scramble onto the wall.

"Oh, my," Francesca said, standing unsteadily.

"Isn't it wonderful?" Elsa said.

"I don't know. I haven't opened my eyes yet," Francesca whispered.

"We'll hold onto you, Francesca," Elsa assured her. Her own knees were still shaky. "Look at the stars. There are so many of them."

"More than anybody could ever count." Matty sighed.

"I think this was the best day of my whole life," Elsa said. She spread her arms wide, wishing she could make everything stay still, exactly the way it was. A breeze was starting up. Her nightgown billowed out from her legs.

"It was a wonderful day," Matty agreed. "We'll be friends forever."

"I hope so," Francesca said. Her voice was almost sad. "My parents have been talking about sending me to school in Boston next year. What if I never see you again?"

The breeze slid over the wall and Elsa shivered. "Don't say that. You heard Lafayette. We'll be friends forever."

"She's right. We'll always be friends, Francesca," Matty echoed softly.

The wind kept rising. Elsa thought about her brother. They hadn't gotten a letter from him yet. She prayed that he was all right. After a few minutes her teeth began to chatter. They made their way back down, then climbed the trellis up to their room. Elsa slid beneath her blankets as Francesca blew out the Astral lamp.

Matty and Francesca whispered back and forth for a little while. Elsa listened to them, her thoughts slow and drowsy.

"Good night," Matty said quietly and Francesca echoed her.

Elsa mumbled a response, sinking into the warmth of sleep.

When Miss Heatherton came to check on them, she saw mounds of petticoats, crumpled stockings and a playing card, lying face up on the carpet, just inside the door. It was the three of hearts.

THE MAGIC CONTINUES...
WITH
LYNNE REID BANKS

THE INDIAN IN THE CUPBOARD

60012-9/$4.50 US/$5.99 Can

THE RETURN OF THE INDIAN   70284-3/$3.99 US

THE SECRET OF THE INDIAN   71040-4/$4.50 US

THE MYSTERY OF THE CUPBOARD

72013-2/$4.50 US/$5.99 Can

I, HOUDINI   70649-0/$4.50 US

THE FAIRY REBEL   70650-4/$4.50 US

THE FARTHEST-AWAY MOUNTAIN   71303-9/$4.50 US

ONE MORE RIVER   71563-5/$3.99 US

THE ADVENTURES OF KING MIDAS

71564-3/$4.50 US

THE MAGIC HARE   71562-7/$5.99 US

ANGELA AND DIABOLA   79409-8/$4.50 US/$5.99 Can

From out of the Shadows...
Stories Filled with Mystery
and Suspense by

MARY DOWNING HAHN

TIME FOR ANDREW
72469-3/$4.99 US/$6.50 Can

DAPHNE'S BOOK
72355-7/$4.50 US/$5.99 Can

THE TIME OF THE WITCH
71116-8/ $4.50 US/ $5.99 Can

STEPPING ON THE CRACKS
71900-2/ $4.50 US/ $5.99 Can

THE DEAD MAN IN INDIAN CREEK
71362-4/ $4.50 US/ $5.99 Can

THE DOLL IN THE GARDEN
70865-5/ $4.50 US/ $5.99 Can

FOLLOWING THE MYSTERY MAN
70677-6/ $4.50 US/ $5.99 Can

TALLAHASSEE HIGGINS
70500-1/ $4.50 US/ $5.99 Can

WAIT TILL HELEN COMES
70442-0/ $4.50 US/ $5.99 Can

THE SPANISH KIDNAPPING DISASTER
71712-3/ $4.50 US/ $5.99 Can

THE JELLYFISH SEASON
71635-6/ $3.99 US/ $5.50 Can

THE SARA SUMMER
72354-9/ $4.50 US/ $5.99 Can

THE GENTLEMAN OUTLAW AND ME—ELI
72883-4/ $4.50 US/ $5.99 Can

Read All the Stories by
Beverly Cleary

☐ **HENRY HUGGINS**
70912-0 ($4.99 US/ $6.50 Can)

☐ **HENRY AND BEEZUS**
70914-7 ($4.50 US/ $5.99 Can)

☐ **HENRY AND THE CLUBHOUSE**
70915-5 ($4.50 US/ $5.99 Can)

☐ **ELLEN TEBBITS**
70913-9 ($4.50 US/ $5.99 Can)

☐ **HENRY AND RIBSY**
70917-1 ($4.50 US/ $5.99 Can)

☐ **BEEZUS AND RAMONA**
70918-X ($4.50 US/ $5.99 Can)

☐ **RAMONA AND HER FATHER**
70916-3 ($4.50 US/ $5.99 Can)

☐ **MITCH AND AMY**
70925-2 ($4.50 US/ $5.99 Can)

☐ **RUNAWAY RALPH**
70953-8 ($4.50 US/ $5.99 Can)

☐ **RAMONA QUIMBY, AGE 8**
70956-2 ($4.99 US/ $6.50 Can)

☐ **RIBSY**
70955-4 ($4.99 US/ $6.50 Can)

☐ **STRIDER**
71236-9 ($4.50 US/ $5.99 Can)

☐ **HENRY AND THE PAPER ROUTE**
70921-X ($4.50 US/ $5.99 Can)

☐ **RAMONA AND HER MOTHER**
70952-X ($4.99 US/ $6.50 Can)

☐ **OTIS SPOFFORD**
70919-8 ($4.50 US/ $5.99 Can)

☐ **THE MOUSE AND THE MOTORCYCLE**
70924-4 ($4.50 US/ $5.99 Can)

☐ **SOCKS**
70926-0 ($4.99 US/ $6.50 Can)

☐ **EMILY'S RUNAWAY IMAGINATION**
70923-6 ($4.50 US/ $5.99 Can)

☐ **MUGGIE MAGGIE**
71087-0 ($4.99 US/ $6.50 Can)

☐ **RAMONA THE PEST**
70954-6 ($4.50 US/ $5.99 Can)

☐ **RALPH S. MOUSE**
70957-0 ($4.50 US/ $5.99 Can)

☐ **DEAR MR. HENSHAW**
70958-9 ($4.99 US/ $6.50 Can)

☐ **RAMONA THE BRAVE**
70959-7 ($4.99 US/ $6.50 Can)

☐ **RAMONA FOREVER**
70960-6 ($4.99 US/ $6.50 Can)

☐ **FIFTEEN**
72804-4/$4.99 US/ $6.50 Can

☐ **JEAN AND JOHNNY**
72805-2/$4.50 US/ $5.99 Can

☐ **THE LUCKIEST GIRL**
72806-0/$4.50 US/ $5.99 Can

☐ **SISTER OF THE BRIDE**
72807-9/$4.50 US/ $5.99 Can

They're super-smart, they're super-cool, and they're *aliens*!
Their job on our planet? To try and resuce the...

RU1:2
79729-1/$3.99 US/$4.99 Can

One day, Xela, Arms Akimbo, Rubidoux, and Gogol discover a
wormhole leading to Planet RU1:2 (better known to its inhab-
itants as "Earth") where long ago, all 175 members of a secret
diplomatic mission disappeared. The mission specialists scattered through time all over the planet. They're Goners—and
it's up to four galactic travelers to find them.

THE HUNT IS ON
79730-5/$3.99 US/$4.99 Can

The space travelers have located a Goner. He lives in Virginia
in 1775 and goes by the name "Thomas Jefferson." Can they
convince the revolutionary Goner to return to their home
planet with them?

ALL HANDS ON DECK
79732-1/$3.99 US/$4.99 Can

In a port of the Canary Islands in 1492, the space travelers
find themselves aboard something called the *Santa Maria*, with
Arms pressed into service as a cabin boy.